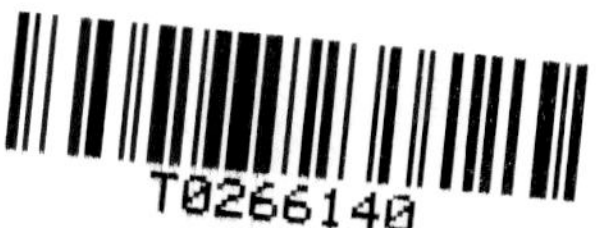

BOB, or MAN on BOAT

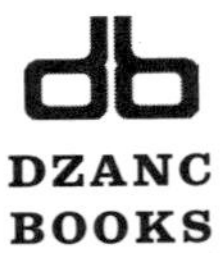

DZANC
BOOKS

1334 Woodbourne Street
Westland, MI 48186

www.dzancbooks.org

The characters and events in this book are fictitious. Any similarity to real persons, living or dead, is coincidental and not intended by the author.

© 2008, Text by Peter Markus
All rights reserved. Except for brief quotations in critical articles or reviews, no part of this book may be reproduced in any manner without prior written permission from the publisher:
Dzanc Books, 1334 Woodbourne Street, Westland, MI 48186

Published 2008 by Dzanc Books
Book design by Steven Seighman

06 07 08 09 10 11 5 4 3 2 1
First Edition June 2008

ISBN – 13: 978-0-9793123-3-5
ISBN – 10: 0-9793123-3-7

Printed in the United States of America

BOB, or MAN on BOAT

a novel

Peter Markus

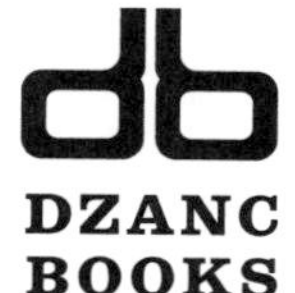

DZANC
BOOKS

for my father
who first showed me the river

and my mother
who told me stories about the stars

In a boat, on a river, lived a man.

Bob.

Bob fished.

It's what Bob did.

All of the time.

Fish. And fish.

Sometimes, Bob ate the fish. But most of the time, what Bob did with the fish was, Bob sold the fish.

It's how Bob lived.

A boat. A river.

Fish.

A man.

Bob.

Look at Bob's hands. His knuckles are rivers. The skin on Bob's hands, fish-scale covered, they look like they've been dipped in stars.

When Bob fishes, he fishes with his hands.

Bob is a hand-liner.

A hand-liner is a fishing man who fishes with his fishing line running through his hands.

Bob does not fish with a fishing pole to help him fish his fish in with.

At night is when Bob likes to fish best. The river at night is the river that Bob likes most.

The river at night is his.

Bob's.

By day, Bob sleeps.

The river, when the sun is on the river, is the river that Bob does not like to fish.

When the sun is on the river, the river gets too muddy with boats that do not belong to Bob.

Bob is a man who lives on his boat.

Bob does not like to step foot off of his boat.

Bob is his boat.

Bob's boat is his home.

Bob's boat, like most boats, it has a name.

Bob.

Its name is.

The word Bob is nowhere to be found painted onto the back of Bob's boat.

But when you see Bob's boat, out on the river, what you would say is, even if you do not see Bob there on it, you would say, Look, there's Bob.

Bob's boat is a boat made out of metal.

Bob's boat is older than Bob.

Bob's boat used to belong to Bob's father.

Bob's father is the man who taught Bob how to fish.

Bob's father was a man who liked to fish too.

But not as much as Bob.

Bob's father, when he wasn't fishing, he was working at the mill.

Bob's father was what we call, in our town, a hot metal man.

In our town there is a mill that used to make steel out of a stone we call ore.

But the mill, our mill, it is no longer a mill that makes steel.

The mill, it has been dark and quiet and with no fire burning inside it since Bob was a young man about ready to make steel alongside his father.

The mill, it's still there, where it has always been, on the bank of the river, shipwrecked and rusting in the riverbank's mud.

The river, like the mud, it will always be.

And Bob will be there on it. As long as there is a river there. As long as there are fish in the river for Bob to fish.

Fish, Bob will fish.

Bob will live.

There he is now.

Say hello to Bob.

Raise up your right hand.

Bob won't wave back.

Bob can't hear you.

No, it's not that Bob is deaf.

It's just that Bob chooses not to hear.

There are people in this town who say about Bob that Bob only talks to fish. That Bob only listens to fish.

I am not one of those people.

Bob does not talk to fish.

That is, Bob does not just talk to fish.

Bob sings to fish.

Listen.

There is, I know, a difference.

I know about this difference because I am Bob's son.

I am a Bob too.

Bob does not know that I am his.

I am his even though Bob does not know this.

I too am a Bob who likes to fish.

By telling you about Bob, I am more of a father to Bob than Bob is a father to me.

But unlike Bob, I do not live to fish.

There is, in this, a difference.

I have a life outside the river.

I have a wife that I love. I have a little boy whose name is not Bob.

My boy's name, it is Robert.

We call him Bobby.

But Bobby's friends, they all call him Bob.

Bobby does not know that Bob is my father.

Bobby does not know that Bob is his grandfather.

But Bobby knows who the Bob out on the river is.

Everyone in this town knows who that Bob is.

Bob is what we call, in this dirty river town, a river rat.

A river man.

Bob is the river.

Bob is this river town's river man.

Bob knows this river better than you and I know that we have ten fingers on our hands.

Bob knows where the fish are in this river.

Bob knows what the bottom of the river is like and where it is that the fish like to be fish.

This river, it is a muddy river.

This river is not the kind of a river that you can see down to the bottom of it even when you are standing in it only up to your knees.

There are people in town who believe that Bob can see all the way down to the river's bottom.

I am one of those people.

I have seen Bob lean over the side of his boat and I have seen him seeing, I have seen him looking, all the way down to the river's muddy bottom.

Everybody knows that the bottom of the river is where the big fish like to be fish.

Even those in our town who do not fish know enough about fish to know this about fish.

Even when Bob is not fishing, Bob is thinking about fishing.

If Bob is not on his boat fishing, Bob is on his boat getting himself ready to fish.

There are things to tend to, there are things to fix, on a boat like Bob's.

Boats like Bob's sometimes leak.

A boat that leaks can sometimes become a boat that sinks.

There is a story about Bob that, one night in April, the wind turned on Bob and came all of a sudden blowing from out of the south and the river, it turned all of a sudden into more like a big lake with seas as big as Bob is tall and that night, Bob's boat, it turned over, but unlike other boats that turn over, Bob's boat, it did not into the river sink.

There is no one I know who was on the river that night to say if this story is made up.

It was not the kind of a night that people other than Bob were out on the river fishing.

The river that night was all Bob's.

The next morning, Bob was seen bailing bucket after bucket of muddy river water out of his boat.

Need a hand, Bob? a few river people called out.

Bob did not look up from his boat.

Bob did not stop bailing the muddy river water out of his boat.

That night, Bob was back, in his boat, out on the river fishing.

The river, that night, was back to being a river and not like being a lake.

When Bob came back in, the next morning, Bob's boat, it was filled up, not with muddy river water, it was filled up with muddy river fish.

You won't ever hear Bob call out, the way some fisher people call out, Fish on!

When Bob fishes, if his lips are moving at all, Bob is whispering to the fish.

What does a man whisper when he whispers to fish?

What does a man like Bob whisper when he is whispering to fish?

What does Bob whisper when he moves his lips to whisper to the river's fish?

Only Bob, and only the fish, know the answer to this.

Some people who fish kiss the fish that they fish out of the river.

Some people who fish say to the fish that they fish, Come to Papa.

Bob is not one of these people.

Bob is Bob.

Bob takes the fish that he fishes out of the river and he fishes them into his boat.

Bob takes the fish that he fishes out of the river and Bob sells the fish, but not so that he can eat.

Bob takes the fish that he fishes out of the river and Bob sells the fish that he fishes out of the river so that Bob can keep on fishing.

So that Bob can continue to live.

Fish on.

Sometimes, at night, when the fish are slow to bite, Bob looks up from the river and looks up into the sky for stars.

Some nights, Bob sees how many stars in the sky he can count.

One night, Bob counted up to two hundred and twenty-two.

That was a bad night for fishing.

That was a good night for counting stars.

Most nights, the fish start biting before Bob can count up to ten.

On a good night of fishing, on a bad night for counting stars, Bob can fill up his boat with more fish than there are stars up in the sky.

Nights like this, Bob's boat is no longer just a boat.

It is a constellation of fish.

Out on the river, out where the river runs out and turns into lake, there is a lighthouse out there to light the way for boats to see by.

There is a man out there who works this lighthouse light.

Actually there are three men out there who work this lighthouse light together.

None of their names are Bob.

None of these men live in the lighthouse there at the edge of the river where the river runs out and turns into the lake.

The lake is big, it is bigger than the river is, and there are ships out there that come from places faraway.

Germany.

China.

Russia.

Duluth.

I don't know how these boats get from over there to over here.

It is a long way.

I would have to look at a map to find this out.

I don't have a map right now for me to look at.

Oceans are crossed.

Canals.

Locks.

Lakes.

Rivers.

Some of these ships, freighters, they come into the river, in from the lake, loaded down with ore.

Others come carrying coils of steel.

There are men who live on these ships.

There are men who work on these ships.

Just like Bob.

When Bob sees these ships coming in from the lake, cutting upriver through the dredged up channels, he knows enough to steer clear of these ships and these ships' big wakes.

Boats like Bob's have been known to turn over in the wakes made by these big ships.

This is not to say that Bob does not fish in the channels made for big ships like these.

These channels are sometimes where the big fish are waiting, and where the fishing is sometimes best.

On nights like these, when the fish are in the channels, Bob goes out there to fish.

There is a light shining out on the front of Bob's boat.

It is green and red.

There is another light on the back of Bob's boat too.

This other light is white.

These lights are not lights so that Bob can see where the river is.

Bob knows where the river is.

Bob can see this without these lights for him to see the river by.

These lights are so that Bob can be seen by ships like the big ships who come in from the lake.

The lighthouse men all know Bob's boat when they look out to see what there is out there at night on the river for them to see.

Sometimes Bob can be seen going out to the lake to fish when he knows the fish are out there waiting.

But even though Bob will go and fish the lake, it's the river that Bob knows best.

Bob is not a lake man.

Bob is a river man.

But even so, Bob knows the lake better than most.

Bob knows enough about fish to know that when the fish aren't in the river, the fish are out in the lake.

And so, some nights, Bob in his boat will go, out into the lake.

Nights like those, the man in the lighthouse will light up his light and say to himself, because there's nobody else there for him to tell this to, Look, there goes Bob.

Bob has been known to sometimes go out into the lake and not come back for days.

Days later, Bob will return to the river with his boat riding low in the river, his boat is so full of fish.

There are limits to how many fish a fisherman can fish out of the river and out of the lake.

There are people on the river whose job it is to count how many fish in a day one fishing man might catch.

Sometimes, on good days, for you to count how many fish there are in the bottom of Bob's boat would be like asking you to count how many stars there are at night in the nighttime's sky.

These people, because they know who and what Bob is, because they know that Bob lives on and lives off the river, they look the other way, to the other side of the river, to the other side of the sky, whenever they see Bob's boat out on the river.

Like the lighthouse men, these men with badges shining on their chest, they say to themselves, There goes Bob.

There goes Bob to fish the fish, they say.

There goes Bob to talk to the fish.

There goes Bob, they say, to whisper whatever he whispers to the fish that he fishes out of the river.

There goes Bob, I say this too. But not just to fish, not just to talk, not just to whisper.

There goes Bob to sing to the fish, to sing them up from the darkness of the river's bottom.

Once, on a visit to a big city, I saw a man on the street who was talking to himself.

I saw another man, too, there in that same city, who was walking down the same street singing.

I was told, by someone who lived at the time in that same city, that both of these men were nuts.

There are people in our town who believe that Bob, too, is a little bit nuts.

What I say to this is, Who among us in this town of ours is not?

Most of the people who I say this to, when I say this to them, they nod their heads to this yes.

Bob is not any nuttier than anybody else is.

It's as simple as this: Bob knows what he likes. And Bob does it, what it is that Bob likes best.

Bob follows his heart.

Bob's heart is a fish.

Sometimes, Bob comes walking into town, lugging with him, hanging from his hands, two buckets filled with fish.

Fish, Bob's lips whisper.

Fish.

It's all Bob has to say.

It's as simple as this.

Fish.

Bob does not have to say it any louder than this.

Fish.

The people in our town who know who Bob is come running up to Bob to buy Bob's fish.

In our town, Bob is known for catching fish when no other boats are catching fish.

A dollar a fish.

Two dollars a fish.

Fifty cents a fish.

When you buy one of Bob's fish, you pay Bob whatever it is you think the fish is worth.

It doesn't take long for Bob to run out of fish.

When Bob's buckets are dangling empty from his fists, Bob turns and walks away, back to the river.

Back to Bob's boat.

Sometimes, when Bob is hungry, Bob will wish that he had a fish left in his bucket for him to fry up for himself to eat.

Back in his boat, his belly as empty as his buckets, Bob will head back out onto the river.

To fish for himself more fish.

When I was a boy, I sometimes used to wonder, How can a thing that is made out of metal not sink? It seemed strange to me then that a metal boat would be able to float.

Most things made of metal do not float.

Most things made of metal sink.

Down to the river's bottom.

Think refrigerators.

Think automobiles.

Think nuts and bolts and screws.

I also used to wonder, back when I was a boy, how it was that Jesus could walk on water.

Every time I tried to walk across the river the river rose up and swallowed me up.

It's true that Bob's father's father was not a fishing man.

He was not a river man.

He was not a hot metal man.

What he was, Bob's father's father, he was a preaching man.

This is my great-grandfather—this man that I am right now talking about to you.

A preacher.

That's what this man was.

This was the man who one day took Bob down to the river and told him the story about Jesus and the fish.

You know the one that says, If you give a man a fish, that man will eat for a day.

But if you teach a man to fish.

I picture this preaching man pointing his finger out towards the river.

That man will never go hungry again.

Bob's grandfather, the preacherman, took Bob down to the river and he told Bob about this.

Some years later I learned that these words, they aren't from the Bible as I had for a long time believed them to be.

It isn't Jesus who is the one doing the talking.

These words, they're from the Chinese, I think.

Or so I've been told.

Maybe it was a Chinese fisherman, or so I'd like to think.

It was these words, whoever it was who said them, that taught Bob how to fish.

To be and to be a fish.

I once saw Bob, at dawn, standing up in his boat, facing where the sun was rising, and what Bob was doing, it looked like to me, it sounded like to me, was he was screaming, though what he was saying, what he was hollering, this I could not hear.

When I told this to a friend in town who is no stranger to Bob, what he said was that Bob was yelling at the sun, that he was telling it to stay where it was, for it to go away, because Bob didn't want the night, and the night's fishing, to come to an end.

The moon, that early morning, that late night, it was full and glowing in the sky.

It must've been a night of pretty good fishing, was what my friend pointed out, if Bob didn't want it to end.

The sun, to Bob, it didn't listen.

The sun is not a fish.

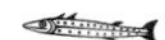

The fish, unlike the sun, listen to Bob.

When the fish hear Bob singing to them, singing to them through the darkness of the river, the fish can't help but take a bite: of Bob's song, of the bait that Bob is fishing with.

Sometimes, Bob takes his fishing hook and Bob digs out the eye of a fish to use this fish's eye for bait.

Most of the time, though, Bob baits his hooks with mud.

Bob is a mud man.

Some men who fish for fish fish with minnows or worms.

We call these fishing men worm men and minnow men.

We call this kind of bait live bait.

But live bait never lives long.

Live bait usually dies before it's eaten.

Which is why Bob fishes with mud.

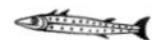

Let me tell you a little bit about a man named Joe.

Joe, like Bob, is a man who lives off the river too.

Joe is a bait man.

Joe sells live bait.

Minnows and worms, leeches and crawdads.

The only kind of bait that Joe does not sell is mud.

If you ask Joe why doesn't he sell mud, Joe will ask you, Who do you know who fishes with mud?

I don't tell Joe about Bob and Bob's mud.

Mud is Bob's secret.

Until now.

This is something else that Bob does to catch more fish than the next fishing man who is fishing the same river as Bob.

Bob likes to spit in the river.

Bob likes to piss in the river.

For luck.

Some nights, the moon is a dead man dragging his hand across the skin that is the river's.

One night, Bob snagged into something on the bottom of the river.

Bob spent fifteen minutes trying to work this snag loose.

This snag, it would not come loose.

After fifteen minutes, Bob was ready to cut his line when the snag finally came loose.

What Bob had snagged, what Bob had dragged his hooks into, there at the bottom of the river, was a man.

This man was dead.

Like Bob, this man was what we like to call, here in our river town, a river man.

This river man, most of us in town, we'd heard the story, how he fell out of his boat, into the river, some time the summer before.

It was now spring.

It was the wake from one of the big shipping ships that did it, that tipped it over, this dead man's boat.

Some say that the dead man fell out of his boat, into the river, while he was doing what he had heard Bob liked to do for luck.

The dead man, before he was dead, he was a fishing man on a fishing boat who was pissing in the river.

Picture this man, this river man, leaning out over the side of his boat.

One hand on his rod.

His other hand holding himself steady.

Fishing for a little luck.

The dead man floated away, down the river, before Bob could fish him up into his boat.

The dead man got away.

Back to the river's bottom.

The fish in this river, when they meet up with Bob, they aren't so lucky.

When Bob gets his hooks into the mouths of these dirty river fish, these fish are soon to be dead.

When Bob cleans his fish, when he guts these fish, when Bob cuts off these fishes' heads, sometimes these fish are still alive when Bob cuts the meat from the bone.

Sometimes, when Bob tosses the fish bones back into the river, to give this part of the fish back to the river, sometimes what is left of the fish will sometimes swim away.

It's like the fish live.

For the river.

It's like the fish live on.

Even when they are dead.

The dead man lives too.

In the river is where the dead man lives on.

Even though he is dead.

Memory is a river.

Bob knew who the dead man was.

Bob knew which boat on the river was the dead man's boat even before the dead man was dead.

The dead man was a man who tried to sometimes talk to Bob, to get Bob to tell him how the fishing was, and what were the fish hitting.

These were the kinds of question people always liked to ask of Bob.

Sometimes Bob would lift up his head, up from the river, and sometimes he would nod.

Once in a while, Bob would whisper some color.

But most of the time Bob would not.

You were lucky if you got Bob to look up from the river.

The river, Bob only liked to talk to it.

To the river Bob told it all his secrets.

The dead man's boat, like Bob's, it was made out of metal.

When the dead man fell out of his boat, the dead man's boat floated away.

The river took it away.

Down the river.

Out into the lake.

It ended up in a place Bob had never been.

Buckstown, Ohio.

On the riverbank of a town that, like ours, is a town that used to make steel.

Two boys, brothers, were the ones who found it, the dead man's boat.

These two brothers didn't know it, at the time, that the boat belonged to a man who was dead.

These boys, brothers, they didn't tell their mother or father about the dead man's boat.

These brothers used the dead man's boat, to fish in, all of that summer and into the fall.

They fished.

And fished.

They kept on fishing.

It was a good summer of fishing for these two boys.

It wasn't until the winter that these boys finally decided to tell their father about the boat.

When the father of these boys saw the boat, he saw that this boat, it was not a boat from the waters of Ohio.

There are letters on boats, there are numbers on boats, that will tell you that a boat is from someplace else.

This father made his sons give up this boat.

The father of these two boys, he picked up the phone. He did some talking into it.

He took two men with badges on their chests down to the river to take a look at this boat.

The men with badges took the boat from there.

They took the boat and found out who this boat belonged to.

It was the boat, they soon found out, of a man who went out fishing one day and then, this man, he did not come back.

This man was the dead man.

The two men with badges on their chest took the boat and gave the boat back to where and to who the boat belonged to.

The dead man's wife.

But the dead man's wife, she did not want this boat to be given back to her.

This boat, the dead man's boat, it now belongs to me.

I bought it.

The dead man's wife, for the dead man's boat, she gave me a good deal.

What do I want with this boat? the dead man's wife asked me.

She said to me, What am I going to do with this boat?

This boat, she said, it doesn't mean a thing to me.

I just stood there nodding with my head.

How much? I said, after a while.

The dead man's wife held out her hands and said a number that I knew was better than fair.

I nodded my head some more.

Then I fished my hand down into my trouser pocket.

I gave the dead man's wife twenty dollars over the number that she said.

Thank you, she said.

When I left with the dead man's boat, I told her I was sorry.

For what? she said.

He's the one, she said, who should be sorry.

She looked off towards the river.

All the time out on that river, she said.

All the time fishing for fish.

Do you fish? she asked me this.

No, I said.

What you want this boat for then? was what she wanted to be told.

I want to learn how, I told her.

I told her, I want to fish.

The dead man's wife looked me right in the eye then and asked me was I a married man.

Do you have a wife? she asked. Do you have kids?

No, I'm not, I told her. I don't.

I didn't want her to know that I did, that I do.

My wife, too, I didn't want her to know about me going out and buying the dead man's boat.

She would have said it was a bad idea.

Nuts is the word that she would have said.

What, do you want to end up like your father?

Do you really want to be like Bob?

I don't know what I would have said to this.

That's a good thing, the dead man's wife told me when I told her that I did not have a wife.

A married man has got no business being out on that river, she said.

If it wasn't for that river, she said.

She said, My Henry wouldn't be dead.

I didn't say anything to this.

I didn't say anything though what I was thinking was that it wasn't the river's fault.

You can't blame the river.

It's the river, is what I wished I had said.

It's the river that kept Henry and men like Henry, men like Bob, a man like me even—

It's the river that keeps us alive.

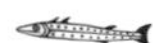

The dead man drowned, as bad luck would have it, because he did not know how to swim.

I did not say this to the dead man's wife though I was thinking it the night I bought the dead man's boat.

I bought it for a song.

What I wish I had said, that night, to the dead man's wife, was that the dead man fell out of his boat, into the river, not because he was standing up in his boat, not because he was pissing in the river, but that it was the moon's fault, it was not the river's fault, that the truth of that night is this: that the dead man was leaning out over the side of his boat because he was trying to kiss the moon's reflection on the river: that the moon, that night, it was a fish floating in the sky, and when the dead man saw it bobbing by the side of his boat, the moon, it looked close enough to touch.

And so he reached out to touch it.

He reached out with his hand to touch this fish.

When he reached out to touch it, the moon, it shattered into a billion pieces. Each broken piece became a star.

So why did I go out and buy the dead man's boat?

I bought the dead man's boat so that I could get closer to Bob.

So I could get to better know who Bob is.

What I know is this: Bob is my father.

I know, even though Bob doesn't, that I am Bob's son.

How else can I say this?

Bob, I wish I could say.

Father, I wish I would say.

Teach me how to fish.

To fish, to catch a fish, this is what you need.

A boat.

A river.

Fish.

Something to fish with.

Some bait.

A net to net the big fish with.

But what about patience?
Bob, is it really as simple as this?

To this, Bob doesn't look up.
Bob doesn't lift his head.
Up from the river.
The way that Bob sees it, the river is all that there is.

Sometimes, when I watch Bob fish, I can't help but believe that Bob is older than the river is.

That Bob is older than the moon is.

That Bob made the moon so that at night he could better see the river.

So that Bob could better see the fish.

This is what a fish looks like to Bob when Bob looks down inside the river to see a fish.

A fish is a flash of silvery light.
A fish is a sliver of milky moonlight.
A fish is a shooting star.
Bob, make a wish.
Get in the boat, fish, Bob says to the fish.

In the boat, Bob whispers to the river.

Like this, Bob wishes.

Bob's boat, when Bob makes his wishes, his boat fills up.

With stars.

With moon.

With light.

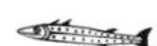

At night there are other lights that light up the river.

There is the light from the lighthouse light.

There are lights from the houses with the people who live inside them.

There are lights from factories along the river that haven't yet shut down.

Nights when the moon is full, it is so lit up on the river that Bob in his boat looks like he is glowing from inside him.

As if Bob is made out of light.

But no.

Bob is a man made out of flesh.

Once, when I shook Bob's hand, there was bone there for me to shake.

I'm Bob, I said, and I stuck out my hand for Bob to take it.

It's true that Bob hesitated at first, Bob looked at my hand, but then he took it, my hand, the way that a fish might look at a rusty hook before taking it into its mouth.

I'll take two fish, I said to Bob.

One for me.

One for my father.

Bob gave me a look.

It wasn't a mean look.

It wasn't the kind of look that makes you want to turn and run away.

But it was a look that says let's get this over with.

Bob handed me two fish.

I took them both into one hand.

I stuck out my other hand and waited for Bob to take it.

When Bob took his hand away, I watched Bob turn and walk away, back to the river.

It was like losing a fish right at the side of the boat.

It was like watching a fish spit out the hook and then disappear back into the river.

The big ones, they say, always get away.

Unless you're Bob.

Bob lives, in his boat, on the river, in a part of our town that is known in our town as Mud Bay.

Some people call it the Black Lagoon.

This is where the river is at its muddiest.

The banks along the river here are muddy too.

There is a dirt road that runs its way down to the river, down to where Bob lives on his boat.

This road is most of the time muddy.

This is a road that, in the mud, cars get stuck in.

Because of this, most people do not use it.

What would they use it for?

To visit Bob?

Bob doesn't want to see you.

If there was a sign posted somewhere along this road, this sign would say, Keep Out.

Don't go any further.

This is my river.

Signed, in mud,

Bob.

I know better than to go down this road.

When I go see Bob, I go by boat.

The dead man's boat.

I wonder if Bob ever dreams about the dead man.

The dead man getting away.

The dead man was not a fish.

Maybe that's why the dead man got away.

I wonder, too, if Bob knew that the dead man's name was Henry.

Or did, to people like Bob, the dead man go by Hank?

These are just some of the things I'd like to some day ask Bob.

My mother, if my mother knew what I was up to, would say to me to stay away.

Stay away from the river.

Stay away from Bob.

He isn't right, is what my mother would say about Bob.

He isn't all there.

Where, exactly, I would want to ask my mother, is there?

Is there a better place for a man like Bob to be, or for a man like me to be, than on a boat on the river?

Why didn't you ever tell him? I asked my mother once.

Why, in other words, didn't you give Bob a chance to be my father?

I was young, my mother said.

She said she was afraid.

Of what?

Of what he would do.

What would he do, did you think?

I was afraid, my mother said, that he'd take you down to the river.

What I wanted to know was, What would be so wrong with that?

In a sack, my mother said, and she looked me straight in the eye.

In a sack tied tight with twine.

In a sack filled up with bricks.

I have a hard time believing what my mother said about the sack.

Maybe because I don't want to believe it.

Maybe I want to believe that Bob would have been the kind of a father who would have taken me down to the river, not to get rid of me, not to give me back to the river, but to teach me how to fish.

When I see Bob out on the river fishing, what I ask him is, How's the fishing?

One time all Bob did was bob his head.

Another time Bob said he had a couple.

When Bob says that he's got a couple, he does not mean just two.

A couple dozen, maybe.

A couple hundred, on a good night.

Sometimes you will see boats on the river bunched up so close to each other that they actually bang together on the drift.

Bob's boat is never one of those boats.

Bob fishes alone.

Bob fishes outside the pack.

Bob fishes the part of the river that nobody else thinks to fish.

I am not the first fisherman to follow Bob around the river to find out how and where Bob fishes.

But the thing with Bob is this:

You can be fishing the same water as Bob and you won't catch a single fish.

That's because Bob is fishing up from the river all of the fish that you can't catch.

It's got nothing to do with luck.

It's got nothing to do with the kind of bait that Bob is fishing with.

It's got everything to do with Bob and with who Bob is and the fact that Bob does not just live on the river.

Bob lives in the river.

Yes, just like a fish.

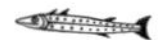

It's true that I've seen Bob fish a fish out of the river with just his bare Bob hands.

Sometimes it's more than just one fish that Bob fishes with his hands out of the river.

It's true, too, that I have heard Bob sing the fish up into his boat.

It's not a song that you and I can hear just because we have ears.

But the fish can hear it.

The fish listen to Bob sing when Bob opens up his mouth and sings to them, Fish, oh fish, come here.

I've seen fish walk across water to get to where Bob is singing to them this song.

I've seen fish leap up at Bob and up into Bob's boat like fish looking to be kissed.

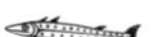

One day I get home from the river.

What my wife says to me when I come in from the river is, I didn't marry a fisherman.

She says, Remember, you have a son too.

Ever since you bought that boat, she says.

She does not finish this sentence.

She goes over to where the sink is and she turns on the faucet.

Hot water hisses against two dirty plates.

I am late again for supper.

I see my son sitting in front of the TV.

He is in his underwear.

He's six.

He is watching a TV show that I do not know the name of.

Hey, buddy boy, I say.

He does not turn toward the sound of his daddy's voice.

What's going on, little man? I say.

He doesn't say anything to this.

Guess what I saw out on the river today?

On the TV there is a clown made out of clay.

I saw this really big ship, I say.

My son looks up at me, away from the TV.

What? he says, though I don't think he's heard what I've said.

A big ship that sailed here all the way from China.

His eyes widen though I wonder if he knows what and where is China.

What about Bob? my son then says.

I wonder what and how much he knows about Bob.

What about Bob? I say.

Was Bob on the China ship?

No, I say.

I say, Bob was on Bob's boat.

Then he says, Is Bob going to go to China?

I guess he does know what China is.

I don't think so, I tell him.

On the TV the clay clown is juggling three clay fish.

Did you catch any fish? he asks.

A couple, I say. Want to see them? One's got some pretty big teeth on him.

Maybe later, he says.

He turns back to face the TV.

Some nights it's hard to get my own son to bite.

In bed, that night, my wife says it again.

I didn't marry a fisherman.

She turns over onto her side.

Her back is to my belly.

Like that, she reaches over and turns out the light.

That night, I have a dream with Bob fishing in it.

In this dream, I am fishing with Bob.

I am fishing in Bob's boat.

Bob is teaching me how to fish.

He is pointing to places in the river where, he says, there are always more than just one fish for a man to fish up.

Then Bob says to me, Hold out your hands.

So I hold out my hands.

He takes my hands into his own.

He looks down at my hands.

I can tell that he is looking.

I look down at his.

His hands are scaled and webbed.

His hands are fins.

I pull my hands away from Bob.

What's the matter? Bob asks me. Haven't you ever shaken hands with a fish?

I shake my head no.

That's your problem, Bob tells me.

Bob turns, then, and just like that, Bob jumps out of his boat.

Into the river.

Bob swims away.

And I'm left alone, then, floating down the river, here in Bob's boat.

In the morning, I boat my boat over to Bob's boat.

Bob is not in it.

I look around for Bob.

Mornings, Bob usually spends cleaning fish.

The sun is on the river.

The sun makes a mist on the top of the river.

Bob, I call out.

My voice is a stone that skips across the river.

I ask a man in a fishing boat if he has seen Bob.

He shakes his head nope.

I go home.

Home, I pick up the phone.

I don't know what or who I should call. Or what I would say if I had to say it.

That Bob is not in his boat?

That in my dream Bob had become a fish?

That afternoon, I get in my truck and go down the road that goes down to the river.

Down to the river where Bob lives.

I want to see if Bob is back home in his boat.

He is.

Bob's boat is back to being Bob's boat.

Bob's boat, when Bob is not on it, it goes back to being just another boat on the river.

I see Bob hunched over, sitting on a turned-over bucket, gutting the guts out of his fish.

The guts of the fish, Bob throws the guts back into the river.

Bob believes that the guts of the fish, when you give them back to the river, the guts turn back into fish.

There are boats on the river with people on them who do not fish.

The river, to these people on board these boats, it is just a place for them to swim in, it is a place for them to cool down during the heat that is the summer.

Summer days, Bob watches these boats and these people speed on by, going to where Bob doesn't know.

Sometimes these boats, the people on these boats, when they motor on by Bob in his boat, they holler out to Bob for Bob to get out of their way.

Bob doesn't holler anything back.

Bob doesn't bother.

Bob isn't bothered too much by these boats.

Bob knows that, in a couple of years, those boats won't be out on the river getting in Bob's way.

Those boats will be put up on trailers, they'll be stored away in somebody's backyard garage.

The people who own these stored-away boats, they'll cover up these boats with tarps to keep them from getting dusty.

Bob knows what keeps a boat from getting dusty.

A boat is like a fish.

When you take a boat out of the river.

It is no longer a boat.

It becomes something else.

A boat is not a boat, Bob knows, unless it's a boat floating out on the river.

Bob's boat is always out on the river.

The only time Bob takes his boat out of the water is if Bob has to fix a leak.

Even in winter, when the river turns to ice, Bob keeps his boat out there on the river.

In the winter, the river becomes something else besides a river.

The river becomes a river made out of ice.

In the winter, Bob cuts out chunks from the ice so that he can keep on fishing, even though it's cold.

Some days it's so cold out on the river, in the winter, that Bob's hands turn to ice.

But underneath the ice, the river is still there, it is still forever flowing.

And so are the fish.

Where the river is the fish will always be.

Where the river is and where the fish are is where you'll find Bob fishing for fish.

This is something you can count on.

Where the river is.

Up above the fish.

There is Bob.

Here is Bob now.

Bob is sitting on the ice on a bucket that is turned over on the ice so that Bob can sit down on it.

When Bob isn't sitting on the ice on a bucket, Bob is on his knees kneeling down on the ice.

The ice here is sixteen inches thick.

Ice this thick is thick enough for a man like Bob to jump up and down on it.

This is ice that if Bob had a pickup truck, Bob could drive it out onto this ice.

But Bob does not have a pickup truck to drive out on this ice with.

Bob does not even have a pickup truck for him to drive into town with.

Bob does not need a pickup truck.

The river is Bob's road.

And a boat is all that Bob needs.

When Bob needs to go into town, to sell his fish, to get gas for his boat, to get whatever else he can't get from the river—a new pair of boots, maybe, or new laces for his old pair of boots, or maybe to get himself something other than water to drink—

Bob walks.

Up from the river.

Up the muddy road.

Into town.

You can always tell when Bob comes into town.

You can always tell where Bob has walked when Bob comes walking into town.

It's the mud that gives Bob away.

It's that trail of muddy boot tracks that begins at the river's edge and ends in the middle of where town is.

Or else these muddy tracks begin in the middle of where town is and end at the river's edge.

Down where Bob's boat is.

It all depends on how you look.

The Bob who walks into town, to sell off his fish, to get gas for his boat, to get whatever else he can't get from the river—a new pair of boots, et cetera, et cetera:

This Bob is a fish out of water.

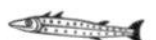

There was a time when Bob wasn't a fish out of water.

There was a time when Bob was just a boy.

There was a time when to Bob, in Bob's boy eyes, the river was just a river.

But then something happened, to this boy Bob.

Down by the river.

Down in the river.

This boy Bob heard a sound.

This sound, it was coming from the river.

This sound, Bob knew, it was coming from a fish.

The river with this fish in it, it was calling out to Bob his name.

Bob, Bob, is what this sound said.

This fish, and the river it was in, it was like it was singing out to Bob.

Bob could see the river—it was the river—but Bob wanted to see this fish.

Bob wanted to hold this fish in his hands.

Bob wanted this fish.

But no, not just any fish.

This fish that Bob heard that day, this fish, it was a fish with his name on it.

Bob.

Bob knew it, that when he saw it, this fish, he would know it, that this fish was the fish.

And so Bob fished.

Bob fished and he fished for this fished-for fish.

Bob caught hundreds, thousands, of fish that were not the fish that he was fishing for.

Some of these fish were the fish Bob ate.

The fish that Bob did not eat, these were the fish Bob sold when he came into town with his buckets filled up to their brims with fish.

Bob caught more fish out of the river than anyone else who fished the river.

Bob caught so many fish out of the river that runs its way through this dirty river town, there were people in town who believed that Bob was fishing the river clean.

That Bob was fishing the river dry.

That there would come a day when there would be no more fish for us and for Bob to fish.

That we would one day run ourselves out of fish.

Bob knew this was not possible.

As long as there was a river, Bob knew there'd be fish in the river to fish.

And as long as there was a river to fish, Bob believed that one of those fish would be the fish that he was fishing for.

That one of those fish would be the fish that called out to him his name.

Bob.

Bob also knew that it was possible, too, that the fish that he was fishing for, it was possible that somebody else who was fishing the river might one day catch this fish too.

This worried Bob more than anything else.

To think that his fish could end up in somebody else's boat, or in somebody else's hands, in some other fishing man's bucket.

Bob did not want to think about this.

Bob could not think about this.

But, of course, Bob did.

It was all that Bob could think about.

It was this that kept Bob fishing.

It was this that kept Bob living, on a boat, on the river, fishing for this fish.

The river, when you see pictures of it that have been taken from a plane, it looks like an S, or a snake—no, it's more like a worm, or nightcrawler, which is what a lot of the fisher folks who fish on the river like to bait their fishing hooks with.

Worms, Bob knows, will catch you some fish.

So will minnows.

Shiners.

So will leeches.

Slugs.

But Bob knows, too, that none of these baits work as good as what Bob baits his fishing hooks with.

Mud.

Nothing works as good as mud does.

Mud is the bait that Bob likes best.

Sometimes, though, Bob wonders if maybe that one fish that he is fishing for, that maybe this fish is looking for something else.

Something other than mud.

Something other than minnows and worms.

Something other than leeches and slugs.

Sometimes Bob wonders that maybe this fish that he is fishing for, maybe it's a fish that's looking for a bait that no fisherman has ever fished the river with.

Nights like those, Bob takes one of his fishing hooks and he sticks it into his finger.

Bob presses down on this hook into his finger until blood comes rivering out.

Maybe this fish that Bob is fishing for, maybe it wants more from Bob than just plain mud.

Maybe mud, to this fish, isn't enough.

Maybe what this fish wants from Bob is the blood that flows, like a river, on the inside of Bob's body.

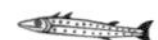

The blood from Bob's fingers hasn't caught this fish yet.

But neither has mud.

Neither has worms and minnows, leeches and slugs.

Some nights Bob doesn't know what to think about this.

He tries to think of something else to bait his hooks with.

Bob has even tried using fish eyes for bait.

Some of these fish eyes look like moons.

Some of these fish eyes have a light shining out from inside them that Bob hopes might catch the eye of the fish that he is fishing the river for.

So far none of the fish that Bob has fished from out of the river have been the fish that he is fishing for.

You'd think that Bob would get tired of this.

You'd think that maybe Bob would throw up his hands, or throw in the boat, and just give up his fishing for this fish.

Those who think that this is possible with Bob, they don't really know Bob.

What I want to know is this:

What is Bob going to do that day when he fishes up from the river this fish?

That day is going to come.

This fish, it'll one day be, out of the river, up from the river, fished up.

Bob is going to be the one to do it.

What we don't know is when Bob is going to do it.

What we also don't know is this:

What is Bob going to do once he fishes, up from the river, this fish?

I imagine Bob will keep on doing what Bob has always been doing.

I can't imagine Bob anywhere else but where Bob is.

In a boat.

On a river.

Is a man.

Is a fish is a fish is a fish.

But what if this fish that Bob is fishing for, what if some other fisherman or some other fisherwoman fishes it out of the river first?

How would Bob even know that this fish was in somebody else's boat, that this fish was in somebody else's hands?

Bob would know it.

It would be like if, for the rest of us one morning, the sun did not up out of the river rise up.

There would be, for Bob, something missing from the river.

A light.

No.

A sound.

No.

A fish.

There are some fishermen in our town and some fisherwomen in our town who know that Bob is fishing for this fish.

Sometimes one or another of these fishermen and fisherwomen will come to Bob's boat holding up in their hands a fish.

Is this the fish? some of them will say to Bob.

Others will say to Bob, Bob, I think this is your fish.

To these fisherpeople, Bob will look up.

Bob will lift his head.

Bob will give these fish that these fishermen and fisherwomen are holding up a listen, a look.

That's all it takes is a quick lift of the head from Bob for Bob to see, for Bob to hear, that the fish that he is fishing for, it is still out there, somewhere in the river, waiting for Bob to fish this fish up, up out of the river and up into his boat.

I don't know what Bob will do with this fish once he gets it.

I don't think he'll eat it.

You can eat any old fish.

But this fish.

This fish will be a keeper.

Some fishermen and some fisherwomen, when they get a fish that is too big to eat, these people will sometimes get these fish mounted and will hang these fish up on a wall on the inside of their house.

Bob hasn't got any walls to hang his fish on.

When Bob gets his fish, I think I know what Bob is going to do with it.

I can picture Bob now, lifting up this fish.

I can picture Bob looking this fish up and down its beautiful fish body, this fish with a song inside it shining out.

I can picture Bob taking this fish and leaning with this fish over the side of his boat.

To let this fish go.

To give this fish back to the river.

So that Bob can be the Bob that he is.

So that Bob can continue to fish.

Go fish.

But we won't know until Bob gets this fish.

Until then, we can only imagine.

Even I can only guess.

Guess what?

There goes Bob now.

There goes Bob going after that fish.

I'm going with him.

I'm going to go after him.

That man.

That fish.

Bob.

What better gift can a son give to his father than the thing that he is looking most for?

Bob, I imagine myself saying.

Father, I might even say.

I've got something I want you to have.

Bob, I have something I want to give you.

Like this, this is how I imagine this, I hand over to Bob his fish.

This fish, when I give it to Bob, it is still alive in my Bob hands.

In Bob's hands, this fish, it is something more than just alive.

This fish, it is living.

It is like trying to hold in your hands the flowing that is the river.

This fish, it is too big for it to fit inside a bucket.

So Bob and I, we carry it together.

Down to the river.

Here, at the river's edge, father and son, we let this fish go.

We stand and we watch this fish swim away.

We do not say anything to each other about this fish.

Then, after a while, we get into Bob's boat.

For the first time ever in the life of Bob's boat, there is in Bob's boat more than just Bob.

It is Bob and his son Bob.

I start the motor.

Bob steers.

Like this, Bob and I, we begin again.

We go out onto the river, for the first time in our lives, father and son, fishing for our fish.

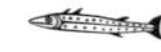

I want that fish.

I want to get that fish.

I want to be able to say to Bob, This fish is your fish.

So I get into my boat.

I get into the dead man's boat.

I've got my bait, whatever it takes.

Minnows, worms, leeches, slugs.

There are things made out of metal—lures, spoons, spinners—that are made to look like fish.

Little fish for the big fish to eat.

I've even got mud to bait my fishing hooks with so that my hooks look just like Bob's.

Maybe I can fool the fish in the river into believing that I am Bob.

Like Bob, to be like Bob, I talk to the fish.

But unlike Bob, when I open up my mouth to talk to the fish, it is more like I am talking to the river.

I don't mind this.

The river is a good ear to talk to.

When I talk to the river, the river listens.

The river never talks back.

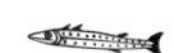

This is my wife talking.

It's after midnight, she says.

She tells me, You said you'd be home before dark.

You said, she says, that you'd be home in time to tuck Bobby into bed.

You know what your son said to me tonight?

I shake my head.

He said that you said that you'd promised him tonight to tell him a bedtime story.

My wife says, You know what else he said?

I don't say anything.

He said, Why does Daddy spend more time with the river than he does with us?

Doesn't Daddy love us anymore?

Doesn't Daddy love us as much as he loves the river?

This is what your son said to me tonight, she says.

What did you tell him? I say to this.

I told him that of course your daddy loves you more than he loves the river.

I told him that in your daddy's eyes, if you were a fish you'd be the biggest fish in the river.

What'd he say to that? I say this to my wife.

My wife says, You want to know what your son said?

She says, You sure you want me to tell you what your son said about all of this?

I nod with my head.

He said, your son, is what my wife says, that he hates the river.

He said, your son, that he wished the river would go away.

I don't say anything to this.

I can't say anything to this.

I must say something to this.

That night, I go into my son's room.

Only his head is sticking up and out from the covers.

He looks more like a turtle than he does a fish.

His eyes, my son's, do not open up even when I whisper his name.

Bobby, I say.

I sit down on the edge of his bed.

I put my hand on his head.

His head, he turns it away.

Is this my son flinching from the touch of his father?

Sonny boy, I whisper.

I put my hand on his chest.

It's me, Daddy.

I'm home, I tell him.

His eyes only halfway open.

I can see that he can see me even though he isn't even close to being awake.

I came home, I tell him, to tell you a bedtime story.

Are you too tired to hear a story?

He shakes his head.

Good, I say.

Once upon a time, I whisper.

In a kingdom far away.

There was a man who lived in a boat on a river.

And in this river, I say, there lived a fish.

I stop the story there.

I don't say anything else.

I don't know what else to say.

After a little while, my son's eyes flitter open.

A fish's eyes, I should tell you, never close.

Daddy, he says.

Did you bring home any fish?

A couple.

Can I see the fish? he asks me.

He always asks me this.

My son, he likes to look at the fish.

He likes to touch the fish.

This is my son.

In the morning, I tell him.

It's late.

I tell him, Close your eyes.

He listens to what I have told him to do.

My son, he is not a fish.

Use your imagination, I say, to imagine seeing the fish.

Then I tell him, Tell me what you see?

What does the fish look like? I ask him.

Is it big?

I can tell that he is looking hard, I can see that he is trying hard, to picture this fish in his head.

He looks like he's having a little bit of a hard time finding a fish in his head to see.

His eyes, I can see, he is squeezing them as tight as he can get them to close up tight.

It's okay if you can't see them, I say.

I tell him, You're probably too tired.

In the morning you can see the fish, I say.

Go to sleep.

But then he tells me this:

I can see the fish.

I see the fish, he says.

I see you, too, Daddy, he tells me.

You see me? I say.

What about the fish?

He nods his boy head yes.

Daddy, he says.

Yes, buddy boy.

He tells me, You are the fish.

I'm the fish?

His eyes close and go back into that other place.

He is seeing something none of us can see now.

I say to myself, I am the fish.

I whisper those words, I am the fish.

Then I say, again, to my son, Go to sleep.

This is all that I can say to my son for telling me I am a fish.

Daddy, he says, after a little bit of nothing.

What's up, buddy boy?

I don't want you to be a fish.

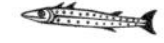

I am a fish.

I am a fish.

That night, I sleep out on the sofa.

I try to sleep but I cannot sleep.

I close my eyes and try counting the fish swimming around inside my head.

There are more fish in my head than there are stars up in the sky.

All night long all I hear is the sound of these words:

I am a fish.

I am a fish.

I am a fish.

This, and the sound of my son's voice saying to me, his father, I don't want you to be a fish.

So I take the next few nights of fishing off.

I don't go out onto the river.

On one of these nights, we go out for dinner.

As a family.

When I order fish and chips, my wife shakes her head.

She says, You and your fish.

For supper on one of these other nights, I fry up some fish fished up out of the river.

My son looks at me from across the table as I am eating up this fish.

I can tell that he is thinking.

He doesn't say what it is he is thinking about.

When I ask him if the fish tastes good, he says that it's tasty.

I fry up the fish in lots of butter.

My son likes to watch me fry up the fish.

He likes to watch me clean the fish.

He likes to watch me gut the fish.

The guts of the fish, we do not throw the guts into the garbage.

We do not throw them back into the river the way that Bob does the guts of his fish.

My wife has a garden out back in our backyard.

I dig a hole in the dirt in this garden and we bury the guts back here.

At the end of summer, you should see it: my wife has the biggest, reddest tomatoes that God has ever seen.

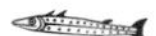

That night, my son wakes up in the middle of the night crying from a bad dream.

We run into his room, turn on the light.

It was just a dream, my wife tells him. It wasn't real.

She pets his head.

I want to know, What was the dream about?

My wife gives me this look that says, What does it matter? It's just a dream.

I dreamed we were fish, is what my son tells me.

We lived in the river.

Hey, now, I say, that doesn't sound so bad.

I tell him, I can think of worse places for fish to live.

I want to know, so I ask him, What kind of fish were we?

He shakes his head that he doesn't know.

Was I a big fish?

He nods his head to tell me yes.

I was a little fish, he says.

And then he says, And you were trying to eat me.

Oh, sweetheart, my wife says to this. I'm sorry, she says.

What I say is, I was trying to eat you?

That's when I woke up, my boy says.

He says, his bottom lip quivering, But I didn't want you to eat me.

I wouldn't want me to eat you either, I say.

I pick him up, give him a big fish hug.

I lick the tears off his face.

You do taste pretty salty, I say.

It hits me one night.

Maybe my son is right.

Maybe I am a fish.

Bob's fish.

The fish that Bob is out on the river fishing for this fish.

Bob is out on the river right now fishing for this fish.

I know this even though I am not out on the river with him.

I am in bed with my wife.

I am trying to get some sleep.

When I close my eyes, I can see Bob, out on the river, out on his boat, fishing for this fish.

When Bob cooks his fish, he cooks them over an open fire right there on the river's bank.

Bob eats fish.

That's all he eats.

Twice a day.

Fish.

And more fish.

There are those in this town who believe that Bob eats the parts of the fish that most of us don't eat.

The head.

The tail.

The bones.

I don't know about this.

But I do know this:

That the part of the fish that Bob does eat, even before he cooks up the fish, is the fishes' eyes.

The fishes' eyes, when Bob eats them, Bob believes, they help Bob to better see.

Down inside the river.

So that Bob can see like a fish.

There are some people in this town who believe that Bob fishes with nets.

How else can one fishing man catch so many fish? is what these people like to ask.

These people who ask this about Bob, they have never seen Bob fish.

These people who ask this about Bob only see Bob when Bob comes into town with his buckets of fish hanging heavy from his wrists.

These people have only heard the stories that some people in this town like to make up about Bob because these people do not know who Bob really is.

These stories about Bob, they are just stories.

These stories are all lies.

This story that I am right now telling you, about Bob, it is not a lie.

It is true.

This is the true story of Bob.

The story of Bob who lived in a boat on a river.

This man who loved and lived to fish.

When Bob sleeps, out on the river, out on his boat, Bob sleeps sitting up.

Sometimes it's hard to tell if Bob is sleeping, or if Bob is just sitting there in his boat not sleeping.

Bob sleeps when the sun is not sleeping.

Bob sleeps when the fish in the river like to sleep.

My son sleeps with the light on.

This is something new.

Ever since he had that dream where he and I were fish.

That dream where I, his own father, tried to eat him.

The light in his room burns all night long.

At night, when I am out on the river, I can see this light shining out.

It is like a lighthouse light.

This is the light that lets me know, when I'm coming in from the river, that I am almost, that I am coming, that I am going, home.

Going home, for Bob, is going out onto the river.

Home, for Bob, is Bob being out on the river, is Bob being out on his boat.

The moon shining its light down upon the river the moon, it is Bob's lighthouse.

And the stars in the sky, the stars are the eyes of the fish that Bob has yet to eat.

The big fish eat the little fish.

This is the way of the river.

Once, when I was out on the river fishing, I reeled in a fish that was too small for me to keep.

It was too small to eat.

I was reeling in this little fish when this bigger fish, it came up and took the littler fish into its mouth.

I reeled in this bigger fish up and into my boat.

When I stuck my thumb into this bigger fish's mouth, to unhook the fishing hook, this littler fish, I could see, it had not been swallowed all the way down into this bigger fish's belly.

This littler fish, it was still alive inside this bigger fish's mouth.

So I did with this littler fish what I would have done with this fish even if this bigger fish had not tried to eat it.

I threw this littler fish back.

Into the river.

This bigger fish, this fish that had tried to eat this littler fish, I threw it into my bucket.

I took this bigger fish home.

Where I cleaned this fish.

Where I cooked this fish.

Where I ate this fish.

This fish, I wanted to teach it a lesson.

There are some people in town who do not think we should eat the fish out of the river.

These people believe that the fish in the river, that if you eat these fish, you will get sick, that you could even die from eating these fish.

I do not believe this.

Look at Bob.

Bob eats fish every day.

Bob eats fish every day, twice a day.

Bob isn't sick.

Bob isn't dead.

Bob is more alive than any other man I know.

Bob does what he loves.

Bob fishes.

Look at Bob go.

There goes Bob now going back out onto the river.

Bob's boat is like a metal fish that swims out over the top of the river looking for fish for Bob to fish.

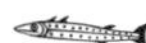

Now, it is raining.

No, it is more than just raining.

The sky is a river that has spilled out over its banks.

In the rain, the river is just a river without any boats out on it.

Except for Bob's.

Bob is out on the river.

Bob is standing up in his boat out on the river in the falling down rain.

Bob is lifting his head up to the falling rain so that the rain hits hard against his face.

And now, it is not only raining.

Now, it is thundering.

Yes, it is lightning now.

Bob is the tallest thing out on the flatness that is the river.

If it is possible for a man to be wetter than a fish, then this man is Bob.

This is that kind of a rain.

Bob is that kind of a man.

This rain, it is a river rivering down.

In this rain, Bob is not just a man, out on a river, out in the rain, fishing for fish.

Bob is a fish.

This is the story of a fish fishing for another fish.

When Bob fishes the river, fishing for fish, he is fishing for more than fish.

There are some fishermen and fisherwomen in town who fish so that they can talk about fishing for fish.

These fisherpeople fish so that one of these days they'll be able to tell you a fish story about the big fish that got away.

Bob does not fish so that Bob can tell that kind of a story.

Sometimes, though, what I do think is this:

That Bob is fishing for the fish that, when Bob fishes this fish up and out of the river, this will be the one fish that will teach Bob something other than how to fish.

I do not know, for Bob, what that something other than how to fish could be.

I can't imagine Bob doing anything besides fishing for his fish.

The river, without Bob out on it, in Bob's boat, fishing for fish, the river, it wouldn't be the same river.

It wouldn't be the same river that it is when Bob is out on this river fishing for his fish.

The river, without Bob on it, fishing in his boat, the river, it wouldn't even be a river.

Now that I am imagining this, the river, this is what I believe would happen to it.

The river, if Bob was not out on it, it would turn, first to mud, then to dirt.

And the fish in the river?

The fish would turn to stone.

But that's not going to happen.

Not to this river.

Not to Bob.

Not to the fish that Bob is fishing this river for.

Bob, when one day Bob finds and fishes out of the river that one fish that will teach him and tell him what to do next, what this fish is going to tell Bob, at least the way that I imagine it happening, is this fish is going to tell Bob to keep on fishing for fish.

And this fish, for saying this, for telling Bob to keep on fishing for fish, the river, it will kiss this fish.

This river, it will throw this fish back.

Back into the river.

Go fish.

Oh, if you teach a man to fish.

The river becomes his home.

The dead man isn't alone.

There are other men who've fallen into, there are others who have drowned in this river that is ours.

There are other men, too, who've gone down to the river, who have walked out into the river, and these other men some of the time did not come walking back.

Even Bob can't walk on water.

Even Bob needs a boat if he wants to cross over to the river's other side.

Except in the winter.

In the winter, when the river freezes over, Bob can walk across to the river's other side.

There are people in town who like to sit out in the cold out on the iced over river and fish for fish through the winter's ice.

In the winter, when the river freezes over, Bob walks out onto the ice by his boat and Bob digs a hole.

Bob digs a hole into the ice.

Through the ice.

Into this hole, Bob fishes.

Up through this hole in the river, Bob fishes up these winter river fish.

Bob fills up his buckets with these fish.

When the fish are fished up out of the river, fished up onto the ice, the fish, with the river still wet on them, they too turn to ice.

In the winter, Bob grows a beard that is white.

Some days, when it's really cold, it looks as though Bob's beard has grown six inches in a single day.

Days like these, there are icicles hanging from the hairs of Bob's winter white beard.

There are other times, though, in the winter, when the ice on the river isn't thick enough to hold a man the size of Bob up.

Sometimes people fishing through the ice fall through the ice.

Into the river they go.

It's not the river that does these people in.

It's the cold of the river.

The heart, in this kind of cold, it freezes up.

Sometimes, the bodies of those who fall through the ice won't be found until springtime.

In spring the river goes back to being a river again that not even Bob can walk across.

Which is why Bob lives on a boat.

A man on a river needs a boat.

A boat to cross the river in when a man is fishing for fish.

Which is why I bought the dead man's boat off of the dead man's wife after his boat was found by those two boys down the way a bit on that other river down in Ohio.

O-hi-o.

Down to Ohio, Bob has never been.

Why go to some other river, down in Ohio, when there is a river right here for Bob to fish?

This is the river where, on the other side of this river, this is where Bob saw and heard the fish that is the fish of all fishes.

There are other fish to fish for in this river.

But in Bob's boat, in Bob's eyes, there is only one fish for Bob to fish.

Sometimes, Bob calls out to this fish by name.

Bob calls this fish Brother.

Brother, Bob whispers, out to this fish.

Brother, Bob sings to this fish.

Bob was born brotherless.

I was born to a father who did not know that he was the father of a son.

Which is what brings both Bob and me out onto this river.

Two fishermen.

Two fathers.

One fish.

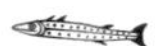

I never did tell you what name I named the dead man's boat.

I named it Bob.

Hold on, Bob, I say.

Bob, I say, don't quit on me now.

Okay, Bob, just a little bit longer.

Good job, Bob, I say.

It's like I'm talking to my father.

Good, Father, I say, every time we make it back from the river's other side.

Bob, the boat, it never says anything back.

It just sits, it just floats, here on the river.

Just like Bob.

Bob is sitting on his boat.

Bob's baits are not in the river's water.

Bob is, at the moment, just sitting there staring out across the river at what I do not know.

Maybe this is Bob thinking.

What is Bob thinking about?

Fish.

His fish.

What if Bob never finds the fish that he is fishing for?

Is this what Bob is thinking?

Or is Bob thinking this:

That the fish that Bob is fishing for, it is somewhere in the river waiting for Bob to find it.

Bob is an optimist.

If you teach a man how to fish, Bob knows, that man will fish forever.

He will never go hungry again.

Such a man is Bob.

Bob is only hungry for one fish.

The fish that is the fish.

There are fish in the river that are considered eaters.

This fish is not that kind of a fish.

And there are other fish in this river that are the kind of fish that you throw back when you fish them up and into your boat.

Come back when you're older is what we say to these kinds of fish.

And then there are the fish like the fish that Bob is fishing for.

This kind of fish, I'm not sure what you're supposed to do with this kind of fish.

To fish this kind of fish up and out of the river, I can only imagine that this might be like coming up to the man who is your father and hearing this father call you his son.

What do you do at a moment like this?

You hold onto it is what you do.

You hold that man in your arms.

You hold your hands onto that fish.

But how long can you hold a fish out of water before this fish starts gasping for breath?

You only get one fish like this.

You only get one father who is your father.

You only get one son if one son is all you've got.

There comes a time when you've got to let go.

There comes a time when you've got to look this fish straight in the eye and then that's it.

It's over.

And the river keeps flowing and flowing.

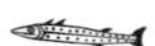

And so Bob goes home.

Bob goes home to his boat that floats on the flowing river.

Bob goes home to the river.

Where Bob fishes for fish.

I go home too.

To be with my son.

I am a father.

My son is a fish.

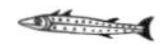

I like to tell my son stories.

My son likes to hear me tell him these stories.

In each story, there is always some kind of a fish.

In each story, there is a man in the story who is fishing for this fish.

This man, I always call him Bob.

The story always ends the same way, with Bob living happily ever after.

After Bob catches his fish.

What my son always says to this is, What happens next?

What does Bob do after he catches the fish?

That's the part of the story, I tell my son, that I don't know what happens next.

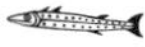

What do you think happens to Bob next?

Sometimes I ask my son this.

My son says that he thinks that Bob, after he catches the fish, Bob gets eaten by the fish.

Bob gets eaten by the fish? I say.

I say to my son, Is that a happy ending?

My son reminds me that this is what fish do.

Fish eat, he tells me.

Fish eat other fish.

So in my son's version of this, Bob gets eaten by the fish that he's been fishing for.

That fish must be a pretty big fish, I say to my son.

It is, he says.

It's this big, he says, and he stretches his arms out as far as he can get them to stretch.

It's as big as the river is, he says.

He says that this fish, it's as big as from where our house is and it goes up all the way to the moon.

That sounds like it's bigger than a whale is, is what I say to this.

It is, he says.

It's a moon-fish.

This fish, my son tells me, it swam all the way down from where the moon is.

That's some fish, I tell him.

I say, That's some story.

It gets even better, my son says.

Tell me, I say.

What happens next?

What happens next is this.

This fish, this big moon-fish, it has swum down all the way from where the moon is to eat up all the fish.

To eat up all the fishermen.

It won't stop, it won't swim back to the moon, until there's nothing left for this fish to eat.

So maybe I should stay away from the river, I say, if this fish is going to eat up all of the fish.

It won't be safe to be fishing the river if this fish is going to eat all of us fishing men up.

And what my son then says to this is that he thinks that might not be such a bad idea.

Three days later, I go out on the river.

Out on the river that night, I see Bob's boat tied up to its dock, but I don't see Bob sitting up in Bob's boat.

I do not, at first, think that something's gone wrong.

I think to myself that maybe Bob has gone into town to pick up some gas to gas up his boat.

But the river, without Bob sitting on it, there's something big missing from this picture.

That night, I fish more fish out of the river than I have ever fished out of it before.

And I know why.

I know that the fish that I am fishing out of the river are the fish that would be Bob's.

But because Bob is not fishing the river, I catch more fish that night—there are so many fish piled up on the bottom of my boat—that it's hard for me to keep count.

That night, I'm up half the night cleaning fish.

The guts, that night, I don't bury the guts the way I usually do out back in our backyard garden.

I put the guts into two buckets.

In the morning, I go with these two buckets of guts, down to the river, and I throw the guts in.

I think about Bob and how Bob believes that the guts of the fish, when Bob gives them back to the river, the guts turn back into fish.

I think about my son's story about the moon-fish that is eating up all of the river's fish.

I think about the river and what would happen, one day, if the river ran out of fish.

I think about Bob again and what would Bob do if the river one day ran out of fish before Bob fished from the river that one fish that he has for so long been fishing for.

I think about Bob's boat and the way that it looked last night without Bob in it.

It looked just like the dead man's boat must have looked when those two boys in Ohio first saw it sitting there in the mud on their river's muddy banks.

So I get in my boat.

I go in my boat down the river to where Bob's boat is.

Bob's boat is sitting there, rocking in the wake made by my boat as I motor up to it, to see if there is any sign of Bob.

There is no Bob sitting there in Bob's boat.

Bob's boat is just a boat.

What I think now, what I know now, is that there is more than just something big missing from this picture.

There is something wrong with this picture.

The river, it is missing Bob.

The river's not the same without Bob out on it.

There's something wrong with this river without Bob fishing for the fish that live down in it.

So I go back upriver, I go into town, and I start asking whoever I see if any of them have seen Bob.

Nope.

Not since last week.

It's been a while.

I bought some fish from him last Friday but I haven't seen him since.

This is what the townspeople who know Bob have to tell me about not seeing Bob.

When I go back out onto the river, to ask some of the fishermen and fisherwomen if any of them have seen Bob, they all say the same thing: nope, not since last week, it's been a while since Bob's been out on the river.

But let me tell you this, they also tell me.

The fishing around here, it's never been better.

I got more fish than I can eat, they say.

I hate to say it, one fisherman says this to me, but this river is a better place without Bob on it.

I give this fishing man a look.

I want to take one of my fishing hooks and hook it through his lip.

I want to take an anchor to this man's head.

I make a fist.

Fish on, this man hollers.

I watch this man set his hooks into the lip of a fish.

This fish, I think, it could be the fish.

It could be Bob's fish.

I pull away before I get a look at the fish that is about to be fished up into this boat that is not Bob's.

That night, I can't sleep.

All night long, I keep picturing Bob, walking along the bottom of the river, looking for this fish.

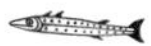

It's true that the big fish who live in the river like to be big fish in the river alone.

It is also true that the littler fish who live in the river like to swim together in the river along with other little fish.

This is true, too, about the people who fish for these fish.

There are people who fish the river who like to fish close to where there are other boats fishing for fish.

It's believed that where there are fishing boats fishing for fish that beneath those boats there must be fish to be fished out of the river and fished up into these boats.

Sometimes, this is true.

But Bob, you will never see Bob's boat anywhere near any of these bunched-up boats.

Bob is like a big fish out on the river fishing for the fish that, like Bob, this fish likes to be a fish alone.

Bob fishes the parts of the river that other fishermen and other fisherwomen believe are dead.

Bob knows that no part of the river is dead.

In Bob's eyes, the river, every last piece of the river, it is alive.

It is alive with fish.

It is alive because of fish.

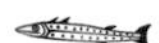

Even the dead man knew this to be true.

Like Bob, the dead man liked to fish alone.

Like Bob, the dead man liked to fish at night.

When the dead man fell out of his boat and into the river, if he'd been fishing close to some of the other boats fishing out on the river that day, the dead man would have probably lived—the dead man would have been saved by some other fisherperson who was close enough to throw the dead man a rope to grab hold of, who was close enough to fish the dead man up and out of the river and then up into his boat.

The only other fisherman out on the river that day who was close enough to notice that the dead man had fallen into the river was a fisherman by the name of Bob.

But Bob was too busy fishing to notice that the dead man had fallen into the river.

Bob had his eyes looking down into the river, at the fish that he was hoping would be his fish.

It's true that Bob did see the dead man's boat not so far away from his own.

The police and the Coast Guard spoke to Bob and asked Bob if he heard or saw the dead man out on the river fishing.

Bob said yes, he did see the dead man's boat fishing out on the river.

Did Bob notice anything strange, they wanted to know from Bob, about the dead man's boat.

What Bob said he noticed about the dead man's boat was that it was drifting out towards the lake.

Did Bob think this was strange to see the dead man's boat going out into the lake?

There are fish in that lake, was what Bob said to this.

When Bob said this, Bob turned and faced the lake.

Bob fishes the lake when Bob isn't fishing the river.

There are people in town who believe that the big fish live out in the lake.

But there are little fish, too, who live out in the lake.

The fish in the lake sometimes come up into the river.

The fish in the river sometimes swim out to the lake.

Bob doesn't care if he is fishing the river or the lake.

Bob knows that the fish that he is fishing for doesn't care if it is in the river or in the lake.

To a fish, water is water.

To Bob, water is water.

The river flows out to the lake.

The river turns into the lake.

All that matters, to Bob, is the fish.

Is the fishing.

Is the fishing for his fish.

Bob is the fish that I am fishing for.

Is there a bigger fish for a man to fish for than the fish that is his father?

I can think of only one fish that is bigger than the fish that is the father.

The fish that is the son.

The fish that is the son is a fish that wants to be fished up from the bottom of the river.

I am a fish.

I am a fish.

When I fish, I fish for Bob.

When I go out onto the river, in my boat, I am not just a fishing man.

I am a fish waiting to be caught.

The river is a bridge to Bob.

In my boat, I float and I drift and I motor on by Bob with the hope that one of these days Bob is going to look up.

One of these days, when Bob looks up, he will see a light that he is looking to see.

One of these days, when Bob listens up close, he will hear a sound that he is listening to hear.

This light, this sound, it is not coming from the inside of a fish.

This light, and the song behind it, it is coming from a boat.

Not just any old boat.

It is coming from the dead man's boat.

And I am the captain, I am the fish steering and standing in the back of this boat.

One of these days, I am going to holler out, to Bob, Bob, take a look at this fish.

I will stand with my arms spread apart as far as I can stretch them, to say to Bob that this fish that I am talking about, it is a big fish, it is a fish so big it is too big to fit inside this boat.

Will Bob even look up?

Will Bob lift up his head?

If Bob knows anything, it is this:

The fish that's already been fished up out of the river, that fish isn't the fish that he is fishing for.

It's not the fish that you can see.

It's the fish that you can't see.

The fish that hasn't yet been caught.

The fish that hasn't yet been named.

When Bob reaches his hands into the river, there is no telling what he might fish up.

And then, one day, up from the river, it is the sun that rises up.

And then, like this, in the light of this light, I see the man that I call Bob.

Bob, I say, when I see that it's him, but Bob doesn't see me.

I am the son that Bob does not know.

I am the fish at the bottom of the river waiting to be fished up.

Bob's boat is a magnet.

The fish in this river rise up, up to Bob's boat, as if they are fish made out of steel.

Bob's father liked to fish but he did not like to fish as much as Bob likes to fish.

Bob's father was most of the time too tired from working to be able to want to fish.

When Bob's father left the mill, after working his shift, he did not go down to the river.

To the bar, not the river, is where Bob's father liked to go.

Bob's father liked to drink.

Like a fish, Bob's father, he drank.

Bob's father liked to drink.

Like a fish.

Bob likes to fish.

Like a fish.

Bob and Bob's father are like two fish.

They are like two fish swimming in two different rivers.

Sometimes, Bob's father drank not just after work.

Sometimes, Bob's father drank before work too.

Sometimes, Bob's father even drank when he was working.

Sometimes, drinking was all that Bob's father ever did.

And then, one day, the mill stopped making metal.

One day, the fires burning inside the mill stopped burning.

One day, the smokestacks of the mill stopped smoking with their smoke.

And from that day on, Bob's father only had one place to go.

No, he did not go down to the river.

He'd go down to the bar.

Where he drank and drank until, one day, after drinking too much whiskey, he turned into a fish.

One night Bob's father drank so much that when he left the bar to go home, he walked the wrong way home.

He headed down to the river.

It was dark out that night.

The moon was not anywhere in the sky shining.

Bob's father walked down to the river in the dark.

When he got down to the river's edge, Bob's father, my grandfather, walked out into the river.

He did not stop walking even when the river rose up past his feet and knees.

He went on walking and walking.

He did not stop walking.

The river, it did not hold him up.

What the river did, the river, like a hungry fish, it swallowed Bob's father up.

Bob's father ended up, three days later, being spit back out onto the river's other side.

The fishing man who found Bob's father stretched out on the river's muddy shore hoped that this man stretched out face down in the mud was only just sleeping.

But no, he wasn't sleeping.

Bob's father was a fish washed up dead on the river's muddy shore.

Bob's father's body was brought by boat back to our side of the river.

It was then driven by ambulance into town where it ended up being taken to our town's only undertaker.

Mr. Lynch.

Unlike many undertakers, ours did not dress in black.

Ours—Mr. Lynch—liked to wear white.

Ours was more like a clown at a birthday party than a man who took care of our town's dead.

But it's not like we had any choice.

Mr. Lynch was all that we had, the only one, the town's keeper of our dead.

If you lived in our town, when you died in our town, it was to Mr. Lynch that you'd go.

Bob's father had made it clear to Bob's mother that when it was his time to go, he did not want to be buried.

The furnace, Bob's father had said.

It's how he lived, face to face with the blast furnace. And it's how he wanted to leave.

Besides, Bob's father had said, it's a hell of a lot cheaper.

Take the money you'd spend on a casket and buy yourself something nice.

So Bob and Bob's mother did what Bob's father said.

They did not bury Bob's father in the dirt of this earth.

They sent Bob's father back, one last time, to the furnace.

Bob's mother took the money they would have spent on buying a casket for Bob's father and with this money in her hand she handed it over to Bob.

He was your father, she told him. I've got the house. So do like your father said, she said.

Go and buy yourself something nice.

Bob took the money from his mother's hand.

Then Bob took from his mother's other hand the container that contained his father's ashes.

Where are you going with your father? his mother called out after Bob.

Bob did not say anything to this.

It was too late to get Bob to stop.

In his head, Bob was already standing at the river's edge.

All Bob needed now was a boat.

So Bob bought a boat.

Bob took the money that his mother gave him and with it, instead of a casket, Bob bought himself a boat.

It was a good boat.

It had a good motor on the back of this boat.

Bob got in this boat and Bob motored with this boat out onto the river.

Bob boated around the river for a while before finally cutting the engine.

Bob drifted a while like this with the motor switched off.

Bob looked up at the sky.

The sky was the sky.

Then Bob looked down at the river.

The river made Bob think of steel.

Maybe because of the color.

It was the same color as Bob's boat was the color of.

A color somewhere in between green and gray.

Bob took the container that contained his father's ashes inside it and then he undid the lid.

Then Bob turned the container upside-down.

The ashes that were Bob's father poured out like smoke and sifted down into the river.

Bob watched for a while as the ashes drifted down the river.

Then Bob saw with his eyes something that he almost could not believe.

It was a fish.

It was a fish leaping up out of the water.

This fish slapped the river with its silvery tail.

Then this fish, it leaped again.

It was hard for Bob to say how big this fish was, though it looked to Bob as big as Bob's father.

And then it was gone.

Into the river.

This fish, up out of the river, it did not leap again.

That night, Bob spent the night out on the river, out on his boat, hoping he would see again this leaping fish.

That was the night that Bob realized that a boat on a river is a good place for a man to be.

A good place for a man to live.

Bob's been living out on it ever since.

This boat.

This river.

Fishing for that fish.

That night, up in the sky, Bob did not notice if there were any stars.

Bob was too busy looking down, into the river, looking out across the river, to see if there were any stars.

What Bob was looking for, looking down into the river, looking out across the river, was that leaping fish.

Bob did not see, that night, that leaping-up-out-of-the-river fish.

What Bob did see, in the river, that night, was the light of the moon.

The moon, that night, it was as big, it was as full, as the moon can get.

The moon, it was too big for Bob not to notice even though he was looking down into the river.

The moon that night shining up at Bob from the river, it looked to Bob like the moon was some sort of a fish.

It wasn't too hard for Bob to see that the moon, it was shaped like a face.

It was not a face that Bob could say whose face that it was.

It was not the face that was Bob's father's.

It was not a face that was even Bob's.

Bob motored his boat over so that he was close enough to get a good look at whose face this face might be.

Bob got so up close to that face that Bob reached out with his hand to touch it.

When Bob reached out with his hand, the moon, this face, it shattered into a billion pieces. Each broken piece, that night, there in the river, became a floating star.

That night, there in the river, there on the river, each floating star was eaten by a fish.

This is how the river works.

Fish eat other fish.
Each star, then, turns into a fish.

If the fish were stars, the sky at night would be lit up, fish-belly white, with light.

A fish is a fish.

Who teaches a fish how to fish?
This is the question.
The answer to this is this:
Fish just fish.
It's how fish live.
It's what they do.
It's just like Bob is.
A man who fishes for fish.

Bob fishes.
Bob is fishing.
Bob was fishing.

Bob fished last night.

Bob will fish again later tonight.

By day, Bob sleeps.

When Bob is sleeping, Bob is dreaming about fish.

When Bob sleeps, Bob dreams about fishing.

Bob dreamed today, as he was sleeping, about fishing for that fish.

That fish, in Bob's dreams, it leaped up out of the river.

Bob dreamed that he woke up on the river.

In Bob's dream, Bob dreamed that the river was his bed.

Bob dreamed that when he woke up from his dreaming, the fish was sleeping next to him in this bed.

Bob reached over across this bed and put his hand on this fish's fin.

Bob shook this fish's fin to try and wake this fish up from its sleeping.

But this fish did not wake up from this sleeping.

This fish was not sleeping.

This fish, it was dead.

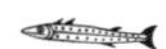

It's true.

Fish in this river die.

It happens all the time.

Sometimes, fish stop breathing.

Sometimes, fish stop swimming.

Sometimes, these fish float up to the river's top.

Sometimes, these fish float on past Bob and Bob's boat.

Sometimes, Bob will fish these floating by fish up out of the river, and Bob will fish these fish up into his boat.

Bob does not fish these dead fish up out of the river and fish these fish up into his boat so that he can sell them.

Bob does not fish these dead fish up out of the river and fish these fish up into his boat so that he can eat them.

What Bob does do to these dead fish that he fishes up out of the river is, Bob guts the guts out of these fish.

The guts of these dead fish, Bob throws the guts back into the river.

Bob throws the guts of these dead fish back into the river so that the guts of these dead fish can turn back into fish.

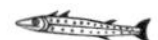

This is true too.

There are some fish in the river that never leave these waters where they are born.

There are other fish, too, who do leave the river waters where they are born, though these fish, when it comes time for them to die, they come back to the river where they were born to do their dying.

Bob's father was a man born and raised right here in this dirty river town.

Bob, like Bob's father, was born and raised right here in this dirty river town too.

Like Bob and like Bob's father, I was born and raised right here in this dirty river town too.

Only Bob's father's father was the only one of us fathers who was not born and raised right here in this dirty river town too.

Bob's father's father was a man who came to this country from a country other than ours.

Bob's father's father came to this country on a boat.

This boat, it was the kind of a boat that can tip a boat like Bob's boat over in its wake.

When, by boat, Bob's father's father came over to this country, this is when this Bob was given his new country's name.

Bob.

It's true that when Bob's father's father came to this country, Bob's father's father did not speak any English.

Some other man who did speak English gave him his name.

Bob.

When Bob's father's father married Bob's father's mother, they had a baby boy and they named this newborn boy Bob.

When Bob's father grew up to be a man, he married a woman who would become Bob's mother. When it came time for them to have a boy of their own, they called this boy Bob too.

This Bob is the Bob who is my father.

This Bob is the Bob who lives on a boat, on the river, and is the Bob at the center of this story.

When I was born, even though Bob did not know a thing about it, I too was named, by my mother, Bob.

Bob.

As my mother once told me, Your name's the one thing you got from your father.

When my son was born, even before he was born, even before I knew if he was going to be a girl or a boy, I took to calling him Bob.

Hey, Bob, how we doing today? I'd say, with my lips pressed against my wife's fish-white belly.

My wife didn't like it one bit, the name, Bob, or the fact that I took to calling our not-yet born child Bob.

What if it's a girl? she said.

We'll call her Bobara, I said. Or Bobbie.

But it's not a girl, I said.

It's a boy.

Because I knew that it was.

It's a Bob, I said.

I said, It's just the way it was meant to be.

Bob.

After a while, my wife gave in.

When our son was born, my wife took one look at him and then she nodded her head.

Robert, she said.

My little Bobby, she said.

We can always call him Junior, she said.

But it's Bob, I said, for short.

Night.

It is night.

At night, on the river, it feels to Bob like he is on a boat floating across the sky.

Sometimes at night, floating on the river like this, Bob feels like he's a bird flying across the sky.

There are birds out here on the river who live along the river's bank.

We call these birds river birds.

River gulls.

River ducks.

River gooses.

River swans.

These are the birds, and these are the names of the birds, who live with Bob on and along the river.

Like Bob, these river birds fish the river for fish.

Hunters who hunt these river birds, when they eat these river birds, these hunters sometimes say that these river birds taste like fish.

We are what we eat.

Bob, if Bob were a thing to be eaten, Bob too would taste like fish.

Fish in the river fish for other fish in the river.

After Bob fishes the fish out of the river, Bob eats the fish that he fishes out of the river.

Sometimes, Bob eats the fish without even first cooking up the fish.

These fish that Bob sometimes eats without first cooking these fish up, these fish that are so small that they fit in the palm of Bob's hand, Bob eats these fish in one quick swallow.

Bob eats these littler fish, fish that fit in the palm of his hand, whole—head, tail, guts, bone.

The fish and everything that is the fish.

These fish, Bob does not cut off the heads off of these fish.

These fish, Bob does not cut off the tails off of these fish.

These fish, Bob does not gut the guts from out of these fish.

These fish that Bob eats whole and in one swallow, these fish, I can picture these fish swimming around inside Bob's belly.

To these fish, Bob is as big a fish as a big fish can get.

To these fish, Bob is as big as a whale is big to the fish that swim in its shadow.

A whale is not a fish.

If Bob were to one day sit down and write down the story of his life, this life story of Bob's might begin something like this:

Call me Bob.

Hey, Bob, I want to one day call out to Bob.

Bob, I am a fish.

I am a fish, Bob.

Fish me!

Fish me up.

But call out to Bob, like this, this, I never do.

Let Bob be, I believe.

Let Bob fish in peace.

Call me Bob too.

I will fish too.

I will follow Bob's boat around the river as long as Bob's boat with Bob on it is out on the river fishing.

I will fish and fish these dirty river waters that Bob has already fished.

I will fish the waters of the river that Bob has already fished just in case the fish that Bob is fishing for isn't, by Bob, fished up out of the river and then fished up into Bob's boat.

If I do fish this fish up and out of the river, I will hold this fish up and out for Bob to see.

Here, Bob, I will say.

This fish, Bob.

Bob, it's yours.

This fish has your name on it, Bob.

Bob, this fish.

I have fished it up for you.

And what will Bob do once I give him back this fish?

Will Bob kiss this fish?

Will Bob eat it, this fish?

This fish, will Bob cut off the head of this fish?

No, no, no to all three of these.

Bob, if I know Bob, Bob will throw this fish back.

Bob will give this fish back to the river.

And the river, the river will kiss Bob back.

Bob, when Bob is thirsty for water, Bob dips his fishing hands into the river and, like this, Bob lifts the river up to his puckered-up lips.

Like this, Bob drinks.

Or, sometimes, Bob will lower his lips down to where the river is and drink the river's water like this, without his hands, just like a fish.

Other people other than Bob, if these other people were to drink the river's water, like this, like Bob, these other people other than Bob, they would likely get sick.

But not Bob.

When Bob drinks the river's water, when he is done drinking it, Bob licks his lips.

Like a fish would lick.

If a fish could.

Lick.

Picture this.

All fish have mouths.

Some fish have teeth.

Some of these fish with teeth sometimes have teeth that you can't see.

But they are there, these teeth that you sometimes can't see.

Give me your hand.

You can feel them, these teeth.

With your fingers, you can.

Stick your thumb into these fishes' mouths.

That sandpaper feeling that you feel—can you feel it?—this is these fishes' teeth.

Those other fishes with teeth that you can see, these fish that have teeth you don't need fingers to feel, do not stick your fingers or thumbs into these fishes' mouths.

Fish are not dogs.

Fish don't bark before they bite.

Fish just bite.

Fish eat.

Fish eat other fish.

Sometimes fish eat other things that these fish think are fish.

Like fingers and thumbs.

There are fish who live in this river with mouths and teeth and bites that are big enough to bite off your thumbs.

There is a man who lives in this dirty river town.

This man is a man who fishes the river.

But his name isn't Bob.

His name is Tom.

There are some folks in town who sometimes call this Tom by Tom's other name.

They call him Thumb.

Tom Thumb.

Thumb is not his real last name.

It is not the name that his father gave him.

The name that his father gave him is Trumbull.

Tom Trumbull.

When we in our town call out to this Tom, Tom looks up, Tom looks over, Tom raises his right hand to say, to us who are doing the calling, Hey, hello, how you doing?

There is something you should know about this Tom's right hand.

It is missing a finger.

No, it is missing its thumb.

A fish took Tom's thumb.

This fish bit Tom's thumb off.

Tom stuck his thumb into this fish's mouth.

To lift this fish up out of the river.

To take out the hook that was hooked inside this fish's mouth.

Tom did not see, he did not realize, that this fish had teeth that you can see.

When Tom stuck his thumb into this fish's mouth, to unhook this hook, this fish bit down hard.

When this fish bit down hard against Tom's thumb, Tom let go of this fish.

This fish, it swam away.

Into the river.

This fish, it was a fish that got away.

This fish, it took Tom's thumb with it in its mouth when it swam away into the river.

Tom raised up his thumb's bloody stump.

Come back with my thumb!

You dirty rotten fish!

Tom says he actually said this.

As if this fish had ears for it to hear.

I sometimes wonder.

How do fish hear?

And this I wonder too:

What would a fish do with a thumb?

Fish don't have hands.

Fish have fins.

Fish have lips.

Some fish have teeth.

I've said this.

This fish had teeth that Tom did not see.

Whenever I see Tom fishing the river, I can't help but think of that fish that took off with Tom's thumb.

How's the fishing? I sometimes say to Tom.

Tom raises his right hand.

Tom doesn't have to say anything else but this.

When Tom raises his right hand, like this, what he is saying is that he is still out on the river fishing for this fish.

Tom is like Bob.

Bob and Tom.

Tom and Bob.

Two men.

Two boats.

One river.

Two men out on the same river in two different boats.

Two men out on the same river fishing for two different fish.

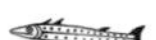

The fish that bit off Tom's thumb, this fish was a bass.

Bass are sometimes called smallmouth bass or largemouth bass.

The bass that bit off Tom's thumb, this fish was a big-mouthed bass.

Largemouth bass have mouths that are sometimes big enough to stick a fist into these fishes' open mouths.

Even though bass have mouths big enough to fit a fishingman's fist inside it, bass do not have teeth.

But the big-mouthed bass that bit off Tom's thumb and then disappeared into the river with it, this bass wasn't like any other bass.

This bass, it had teeth on the inside of its mouth.

It bit on a bass-bait, Tom once told us.

It hit like a bass hits, Tom also explained.

But when Tom fought and brought this fish in close to his boat and when he reached down to it, when this Tom reached down with his right hand and stuck his thumb into this fish's mouth, in order to lift this fish up and into his boat, this is when Tom noticed that this fish—this bass—it had the body of a fish that is called a pike.

A pike is a fish known for the size and for the sharpness of its teeth.

Pike have teeth that even a man born blind would be able to see.

By the time Tom noticed that this bass had teeth like a pike, that this bass actually had the body of a pike—long and thin and spotted—it was too late.

Tom had already stuck his thumb into the mouth of this fish.

When Tom lifted this fish up out of the river, that's when this fish bit down hard and then took off, back into the river, with Tom's thumb dangling like a lure from its mouth.

That's when Tom raised his right hand and called out to this fish, Come back here with my thumb!

This fish, it didn't listen.

This fish, like Bob and his fish, Tom's been fishing for this fish ever since.

This fish's mother must have been a bass.

This fish's father, it must have been a pike.

Or maybe this.

Maybe this fish's mother was a pike and maybe this fish's father was a bass.

It's impossible to know for sure which was which.

Which fish was which.

One thing, though, for sure, is this:

This fish had inside its big-mouthed mouth teeth that were big, teeth that were sharp and sharp enough for this fish to bite off a thumb from the rest of the fingers.

Just ask Tom.

Once Tom tells you this story of the fish that took off his right thumb, Tom will also tell you this.

My name is Tom.

Tom Trumbull.

When this Tom tells you this, he will hold out to you his right hand for you to shake it.

Don't be afraid.

Shake it.

Because when you do, when you take into your hand Tom's thumbless right hand, that's when Tom will tell you this.

It was a fish.

A fish, I say.

It was a fish, Tom will tell you.

And when Tom tells you this, Tom will raise up this hand of his right along with yours.

It was a fish that gave me this.

Tom will say, It was a fish that gave me my name.

Call me Tom, Tom will then tell you to say.

Tom Thumb Trumbull, he will say.

Or just plain old Thumb for short.

That fish that Bob is fishing for, Bob can't say for certain what kind of a fish this fish is.

Is it a walleye?

A pike?

Is this fish of Bob's a bigmouth bass, a fish that is sometimes called a bucketmouth?

Or maybe a catfish?

A dogfish?

A carp?

Or maybe a muskie, which is also a kind of a pike?

Or how about a steelhead?

A steelhead is a kind of a trout.

Or a sturgeon?

Sturgeons are bottomfeeders.

Like catfish are and dogfish are and carp.

Sturgeon can live to be over a hundred years old.

What if this fish that Bob is fishing for lives to outlive Bob?

What if Bob dies before Bob fishes this fish up and out of the river?

Then what?

What would we do without Bob?

When I say we I mean this: me and you and the river and the fish.

Us.

We need Bob.

We need Bob just like Bob needs to be fishing for this fish.

In the end, it doesn't really matter what kind of a fish this fish is that Bob is fishing for.

A fish is a fish.

Is a fish.

If a fish is a fish is a fish, why is it that so many fish are called by so many different names?

Rock bass and walleye, crappie and trout.

Catfish and dogfish, white bass and carp.

Muskie, sturgeon, steelhead, pike.

Largemouth and smallmouth, suckers and browns.

Sheepshead, sunfish, bluegill, shad.

What kind of a fish is the fish that Bob is fishing for?

Only Bob knows what kind of a fish this fish is.

When Bob fishes this fish up out of the river and up into his boat, Bob will know that this fish is his.

That this fish is Bob's fish.

Bob's fish is—there is no other way to say this—Bob's fish.

Bob's fish is its own kind of a fish.

It is a bobfish.

When Bob fishes this fish up into his boat, we can add bobfish to our list of fish names.

Wait.

I almost forgot.

I forgot to mention perch.

A perch is a kind of a fish that it too belongs on our fish list of fish names.

It is, in my eyes, perch, the best eating of all of the fish that you can catch.

Trust me on this.

Batter the perch up in flour.

Fry the perch up in butter.

The littler the perch is, the better-tasting the perch.

You can never eat too much perch.

Eat perch every day.

Until you become a fish.

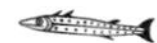

Bob once had a dog that Bob called Dog.

Bob never bothered to give this dog a name other than plain old Dog.

Dog.

Bob and his dog, Dog.

Why give a dog a name, was what Bob figured, when all a dog really wants is a bone.

Bob gave Dog lots of bones.

Bob did not give Dog the bones of chickens or pigs or cows.

Bob gave Dog the bones of fish.

Bob would toss these fish bones out into the river and tell Dog to go fetch.

Dog, Bob would say. Go fish.

Dog would take to that dirty river water like Dog was half-part dog and half-part fish.

Sometimes, the bones of the fish that Bob would throw out into the river, at times these bones would, from Dog, swim down the river away.

One time Dog kept on swimming after those swimming away from him fish bones and Dog never made it back to Bob's boat.

Bob watched Dog swim away, just like a fish, and not once did Bob make a sound with his mouth for Dog to come swimming back.

Bob knew that Dog knew what Dog wanted.

Dog kept going.

Dog kept on after those bones.

Bob is like Dog.

Like Dog, Bob keeps on going.

Bob keeps on fishing for his fish.

I sometimes wonder how far will Bob go.

Will Bob do like Dog did that day?

Will Bob, one night, go out fishing for his fish and then, from the river, not come fishing back?

It's not that Bob wants to see this fish of his that he is fishing for dead.

It's not, for Bob, about Bob killing this fish.

What Bob wants, what keeps Bob fishing for this fish, is for Bob to see this fish alive.

What Bob wants is to feel the life of this fish, the fight of this fish, tugging on the end of his line.

To feel the pull of this fish.

To feel the pull of this fish pulling at Bob like this fish is trying to pull Bob home.

Down to the bottom of this river.

To fish this fish out of the river and then up onto the bottom of Bob's boat.

To lift this fish up with his fingers by the blood-red gills of this fish.

To hold this fish up for all of us fishing on the river to see.

To look this fish square in its fish eye.

This would be, for Bob, more than what Bob would ever want.

It's the feel of the fish that Bob most wants from this fish.

To feel, with Bob's hands, with his fish heart, that the fish is there, that this fish is a fish that is.

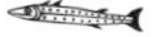

It is hard for Bob to sit on his boat and for Bob to not be fishing.

Which is why when you see Bob out on the river sitting in his boat, you can be sure that Bob is not just there in his boat sitting.

What Bob is doing is, Bob is fishing in his boat.

Bob is sitting in his boat, Bob is drifting down the river, Bob is fishing for his fish.

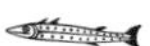

The river that is the river at night.

At night, the river, it is not the river that is the river that is there when it is day.

During the day, when the sunlight is lighting upon it, out on the river, there are boats out on the river that are boats other than the boat that is Bob's.

These other boats are boats other than the boat that is Bob.

At night, the river is Bob's.

At night, the river is Bob.

That is the difference.

That is why the river at night is not the same as the river that is the river by day.

The sky with the sun in it is not the same as the sky with the moon and the stars.

The day river is not the same as the night river.

The night river is Bob's.

The fish that Bob is fishing for, Bob believes that this fish, it is a night fish.

It is a star fish.

It is a moon fish.

Like Bob, by day, this fish sleeps.

This fish, like Bob, by day, this fish is a fish that does not like to fish.

Sometimes, Bob likes to think of this fish as a brother.

If this fish that Bob is fishing for, if this fish is Bob's brother, I can't help but think this:

My uncle is a fish.

Call him Uncle.

Uncle Fish.

Or the uncle that isn't really an uncle.

This uncle, though, that is a fish.

This fish that is a brother to Bob.

A brother to Bob who is a father who does not know he is a father.

Father, I want to say to Bob.

Who am I to say that this fish isn't really an uncle?

Uncle, I want to say to this fish.

I want to take this fish by the fin.

I want to stand this fish face to face with my father.

Stand this fish face to face with Bob.

I want to say, to this fish, This is your brother.

This is Bob.

It's been too long, I want to say.

I want to know too what Bob will do when he stands face to face, facing off with this fish.

What will Bob say?

Will Bob say anything?

Will Bob make with his mouth a sound?

That is the question.

I hope the answer, from Bob, will be this:

This is the fish.

This is the fish.

This is the fish.

But what if this fish isn't the fish that Bob has been fishing for?

You know the answer to this.

Bob will keep fishing for that fish.

In a boat, on a river, lived a man.

How long has it been?

How long, that is, has Bob been fishing for this fish?

It's been.
That's how long it's been.

Been fishing.
Gone fishing.
Going fishing.
Be back when.
Be back whenever.
Be like Bob.
Go fish.
Fish after dark.
Fish in the dark.
Fish through the dark.
Be alive.
Be like Bob.
Be a fish.
Fish on.
Live fish.
Live to fish.
Bob lives.
In a boat.
On a river.
A man.
A fish.
Bob.

BOB, or MAN on BOAT

There's only one fisherman who fishes this river who is known by the name of Bob.

That Bob is Bob.

Our Bob.

My Bob.

The Bob who is my father.

My name is Bob too.

You know this.

I've told you this.

But I am better known, to those who know this river, to those who fish this river, by the name Bobber.

A bobber is what some fisherpeople use so they can see when a fish is biting on the other end of your line.

The end of the line where the hook is.

The end of the line where the bait is.

The end of the line that, when you look down into the water, this is the end that you can't see.

When you look down into the river, you can't see bottom.

Only the fish in the river know what the river's bottom looks like.

Bob likes it like that.

Bob likes to imagine what bottom looks like.

Bob likes to close his eyes.

When Bob closes his eyes, when Bob imagines the river's bottom, what Bob sees is the belly of a fish.

A fish that is bigger than the river is.

A fish that is bigger than the sky is.

A fish that is waiting, one of these days, to rise up to the river's top.

This is the fish.

This is the fish that Bob is fishing for.

This fish.

It lives on the river's bottom.

This fish.

It is the river bottom.

Bob fishes with his hands.

With his hands, Bob feels for his fish.

Bob feels for the river.

In Bob's head, Bob reaches down and drags his hand down along the bottom of the river.

When Bob fishes, Bob does not look up.

When Bob fishes, Bob fishes looking down into the darkness of the river.

Bob, even when Bob's eyes are closed, or when he is looking down into the river's dark, Bob can still see the stars.

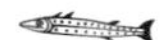

A bobber Bob does not fish with.

It's true that a bobber can help you see that a fish is on the other end of the line biting.

That a bobber bobbing up and down lets you know that there is a fish down by your hook nibbling at your bait.

Bob doesn't need the help of a bobber.

Bob doesn't want any help.

It's also true—and Bob is not alone in believing this—that a bobber can get in the way.

Some fishing men, like Bob, they believe that the fish can see the bobber.

When you fish, you want to be like the river's bottom.

Like a fish down at the river's bottom.

To be a fish in the river.

That's what Bob wants.

To be a fish and not to be seen.

See Bob fish.

Bob's right hand moving up and down, up and down.

This is Bob's hand moving Bob's bait.

Bob's bait moves up and down along the river's bottom.

The river's bottom is where Bob believes that Bob's fish is living.

If Bob believes that Bob's fish is down there along the river's bottom, then Bob's fish is down there, down along the river's bottom.

In the river Bob believes.

The other fish in the river keep getting in Bob's way.

The other fish keep getting in between Bob and this fish that Bob is fishing for.

Bob does not want to fish up from the river these other river fish.

Bob is not fishing the river to fish for these other kinds of fish.

These other fish, when Bob fishes them up from out of the river, Bob keeps them, these fish, Bob does not throw these fish back, because he knows that he can sell them.

If Bob threw these other fish back into the river, then these other fish would still be in the way, they'd still get in between Bob and that fish that Bob is fishing for.

To this fish, Bob is faithful.

If this fish were Bob's wife, Bob would be called a good husband.

Bob would be a good catch.

And if this fish were Bob's son, Bob would be considered a good father.

As it is, Bob is, to his fish, a good fisherman.

A good fish man.

A good fishing man.

Know this:

When you catch a big fish, what you say when you fish this big fish into the boat is, you say:

This fish is a good fish.

A keeper is what you call this fish.

But smaller fish are good fish too.

These smaller fish, these fish we call good eaters.

These not-so-big fish fry up in a pan real good.

Out on the river, it is always good.

Even when the fishing's not so good, out on the river, the river is always good.

Good is a good word to use when you're out on the river.

When you're talking about a fish.

Know this too.

There is no such fish as a bad fish.

All fish are always good.

But a boat.

A boat is not a fish.

There are good boats and there are bad boats.

Bob's boat is a good boat because it is a boat that floats.

It is a boat that holds Bob up.

But there are some boats that leak.

There are some boats that take on water.

There are some boats that, down to the river bottom, these boats sometimes sink.

Like stones that disappear down and down into the river's dark.

There are some riverfolks who know Bob who say about Bob that what Bob is looking for is a stone that floats.

A fish that doesn't exist.

Or maybe what Bob is looking for is this:

A fish that walks on water.

What I say to this, what I say about Bob, is this:

Bob is Bob, I say.

I also say this: that in Bob's eyes, in Bob's heart, there is a fish that is more than just a fish.

There is no such fish that is just a fish.
Every fish is a beautiful fish.
Every thing that is beautiful in this world is a fish.
The moon is a fish.
The river is a fish.
The stars in the sky.
The stones in the river.
The mud on the river's bank.
Fish.
Fish.
Fish.

Starfish.
Stonefish.
Mudfish.

Bobfish.

This is the fish in the river—this is the fish in the world—that I am fishing for.

Question for Bob:
Why a fish?

Answer from Bob:

Why not a fish?

To fish.

A fish.

It is as simple as this.

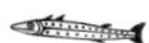

There is no other way for me to say this.

It happens again.

Bob is gone.

Bob is gone again.

Bob is gone fishing is what you must be thinking.

So what?

What's the big deal?

I'll tell you what the big deal is.

The big deal is this:

Not only is Bob gone.

But Bob's boat is gone now too.

Bob's boat is gone and Bob's boat, it hasn't come back.

This is not like Bob.

This is not like Bob's boat.

It's true, Bob likes to go out in his boat fishing all night long, but Bob likes to be back in by morning.

The morning has come and gone and it has come and gone again twice since Bob has been gone out fishing for his fished-for fish.

I've gone looking, all up and down this river, the past two days, looking for Bob.

I've gone looking for Bob out into the lake.

I've asked about Bob all around the river.

I've asked about Bob all around the lake.

I've asked the captains of ships.

I've asked the three keepers of the lighthouse.

Have any of you seen Bob?

All heads shake no.

No, no one has seen the likes of Bob since three days before today.

Today is Sunday.

On Sundays, the river is always thick with boats.

Some of these boats are boats out on the river fishing for fish.

Others of these boats are not on the river fishing for fish.

These other boats out on the river are just out on the river being just boats.

There are people in this world who like to ride up and down on the river on their boats.

These people like the river just because the river is a river.

It doesn't matter to people like this that there are fish living in the river.

These people who like to ride up and down on the river in their boats, most of these folks don't know about Bob.

To these people, Bob is just another fishing man, Bob is just another fishing boat fishing on the river.

These folks don't know the Bob that we know.

Did you know this about the river?

There are places on this river, on days like today, when you can walk across the river jumping from boat to boat.

This kind of a river is, in Bob's eyes, a river not worth pissing his piss in.

This is my river, Bob sometimes wanted to yell this out to these boats.

Go find yourselves some other river to fish or not to fish.

On days like this, Bob would sit in his boat and Bob would wish they would all just go away.

By Sunday night, Bob's wish, it would be answered.

These other boats bogging up Bob's river would all go back to where they came.

And the river, that river that Bob loved best, the river with Bob's boat fishing on it, like a good dog, this river, as day turned to night, this river would come right back.

Every boat on this river that knows about this river knows who I am speaking about when I ask about Bob.

There is only one Bob on this river.

There is only one boat on this river that is the boat that is Bob's.

There is only one boat on this river that is the boat that is Bob.

Bob is what makes Bob's boat what Bob's boat is.

I've seen other boats that look like Bob's, but I haven't seen the boat that is Bob.

You know Bob? I say.

I say, I'm looking for Bob, I say.

Nope, nope, we haven't seen him, they say.

We saw him head out on the river last week, say a few others.

We used to see him out here on his boat every day, say some others still.

Check the lake, they say.

They look out past the lighthouse.

They look out towards the lake.

They say, That's where the big fish are.

Where the big fish are, they tell me, that's where Bob might have gone out fishing.

Yes, I say, I know, but the lake is big.

Looking for Bob out on the lake would be like Bob looking for the fish that Bob has been looking for.

These folks nod their boat-bobbing heads, yes, that's true.

We don't know what else to say.

The moon at night goes from halfway to whole.

It gets a little bit darker every day.

In the mornings, the sun rises.

At night, the sun sets.

But Bob is still gone.

Gone where is what I want to know.

Gone fishing is all I know.

So go fish, I tell myself.
Go fish, Bob.
Go fish Bob, Bobber.
It is the river that tells me this.
Bob is a fish, it whispers.
Bob is a fish.

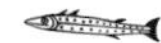

When you fish for fish, you do not see the fish you are fishing for until you fish the fish up and out of the river.

But still, even though you cannot see the fish, you know that the fish are there.

You believe this.
Somewhere.
In the river.
Under the river.
The fish are there.
A fish is near.
So I believe.
I believe that Bob is here.
Bob is there.
Somewhere.
On the river.
In a boat.
There lives a man.
There fishes a man.
Bob.

Even though I do not see Bob.
I know that Bob is here.
I keep on fishing.

Go fish.

To fish.
To fish the fish that is more than a fish.
We fish.
We are fishing.
We fished.
We kept on fishing.
We fished until there was nothing left to fish.

Once upon a time there was a river.
Once upon a time there was a fish.

Once upon a time there lived a man.
Once upon a time there lived a fish.

The man who lights the lighthouse light tells me that he dreamt a dream last night about Bob.

What was the dream about? I ask.

In my dream, the lighthouse man says, Bob was a fish.

Bob was walking across the water.

He was heading out towards the lake.

So I go out onto the lake.

I don't stop until I cross into the waters of Ohio.

When I cross into the waters of Ohio, I come across two boys fishing a river called the Maumee.

I ask these two boys if they happened to come across a man who looked like he might be named Bob.

They ask me have I checked the mud.

The mud? I say.

I say, What would a man named Bob be doing there?

The mud, one boy says, is where the river ends.

Mud, the other boy says, is where something other than water begins.

I nod my head.

Then I give these two boys a look.

These two boys look like boys but what they are, I can see, is they are more than just boys.

These boys, they are brothers.

There is, I know, a difference.

I take back that look.

I turn back towards the lake.

Good luck, the one brother says.

Then the other brother spits.

He spits into the river.

He spits into the river for luck.

I'll take whatever good luck I can get.

The lake is big.

On the lake, after Ohio, comes New York.

Below New York, on the lake, is Pennsylvania.

Bob could be anywhere or he could be nowhere in between.

I go in my boat back to where my looking for Bob began.

I head back to where Bob is a man who lives in a boat on a river.

On a river, in a boat, fished a man.

Call us Bob.

It rains.

It rained.

It is raining.

Rain, and then more rain.

When it rains, it rains a river.

In the rain, the river becomes more than a river.

The river, in the rain, becomes a lake.

In the rain, on the lake, it is hard for me to see.

In the sky there is a star that sailors use to find which way is north.

I don't know which star is which.

I do not know which way is north or which way is south.

I get lost.

I end up running out of gas.

I drift until night turns to day.

There are more stars than there are heartbeats.

I tell myself, This is what heaven must be like.

I don't know why I think this but I do.

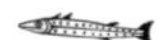

That night, in the rain, with my boat drifting on an easterly drift, I drift off to sleep.

I dream about Bob.

In this dream, Bob pulls up to my boat in his boat.

Bob tells me to come aboard.

I do as Bob says.

When I come aboard Bob's boat, Bob's boat, it starts to sink.

We are up to our knees sinking.

Bob, I say to Bob.

Abandon ship.

I do as I say.

I swim over to where my boat is.

My boat, it is a boat that is not sinking.

I climb up into my boat.

Over here, I say to Bob.

I throw Bob a rope.

In my hands, the rope turns to light.

Bob lets the rope go past him.

Then Bob waves and walks away.

Across the river, Bob walks.

On top of the water, I watch Bob walk.

Like this, Bob is walking.

Back to the other side.

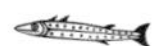

Bob walks and he walks and he keeps on walking.

Bob keeps on walking until Bob is nothing but a sound.

Bob is nothing but the sound that the river sometimes makes when a stone is skipped across it.

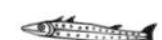

I go home because I don't know where else to go.

I haven't been home in days, in nights.

I've been out on the river, these days and nights, looking for Bob.

I tell this to my son who asks me where have I been.

My son says he thought his daddy was dead.

He says that his mother told him that the river took Daddy away.

Just like the river took Bob, I say, to myself.

I'm not gone, I say so to my son.

I say, Daddy's right here.

Don't go back on the river, my boy says to me then.

I tell my boy I won't.

This, I can tell you, is a lie.

In the morning, first thing, I go out on the river.

I go out looking for Bob.

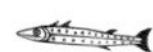

Let me tell you too.

This is a fish story that does not end.

This is the story of Bob.

Remember his hands.

His knuckles are rivers.

The skin on his hands, fish-scale covered, it looks like they've been dipped in stars.